DA...
ST...

Valentina Luellen

A sequel to Lord of Darkness

MILLS & BOON LIMITED
ETON HOUSE   18-24 PARADISE ROAD
RICHMOND   SURREY   TW9 1SR

*First published in Great Britain 1989
by Mills & Boon Limited*

© Valentina Luellen 1989

*Australian copyright 1989
Philippine copyright 1989
This edition 1989*

ISBN 0 263 76423 0

*Set in Times Roman 10½ on 12¼ pt.
04-8905-65691 C*

Made and printed in Great Britain

CHAPTER ONE

THE SOLAR was full of afternoon sunshine flooding across the pale green and blue marble floor, spreading like liquid gold over the plumage of the parrot dozing in the cage beside the door, deepening the honey-coloured Persian rugs scattered everywhere to warm orange, touched with the red glow of the approaching sunset. Pewter and silver plate filled the shelves of the long dresser beside one of the Byzantine arches which curved over the windows.

The walls were hung with tapestries from Syria and Egypt. Warriors clashed swords with warriors against a brilliant yellow background; men in long, flowing embroidered robes sat astride horses with streaming manes, falcons on their wrists, pride blazing from the dark faces.

On one of the sofas low on the floor in the way favoured in the East, Alisandre sighed and rested her head back against a bright-coloured cushion. The infant at her breast continued to suckle hungrily, and she smiled, her sapphire eyes full of tenderness and love as she gazed down at the mass of golden curls. Every day he looked more like Rollo, with the same pale green eyes which pierced her soul when she looked into them. And already he was showing some of the stubborn traits her husband possessed. He would

5

allow no one but his mother to feed him, wailing angrily if he did not recognise the arms which held him or the gentle voice crooning to him—and how he loved his food! He demanded every moment of her time. Yes, she decided, he was growing to be the image of his father—and she would not have had it any other way!

That morning she and Rollo had ridden together, as they had done for weeks past. They revelled in the freedom brought about by the peace between the Christian and Moslem forces who had strived so desperately to take Jerusalem, that most sacred of cities, for one religion only to rule supreme in this land.

Rollo had learned to live with two worlds, as she had. Here, it was never cold. Here she belonged. They all did. The cold she felt, which penetrated her bones at night, even when she lay alongside her husband, was caused not by the weather, but by a hidden fear lingering deep inside her. If she left this place, could she adapt to another? This was their home, where they could be themselves. She could be Karin, the captive, or Alisandre, the rescued Christian woman who had married Rollo, Duke of Aquitaine. Here she would not displease him. And he could be her lord—her master—her husband—her lover—and enjoy all that she had to offer him.

She accepted that they must return to England to claim the estates of her dead father. The king himself, Richard Coeur-de-Lion, had decreed it should be so— so that if she wished, after being held a Moslem captive since the fall of Jerusalem in 1187, she might decide for herself where her future lay. As if she really had a choice! It was at the side of Rollo, her Lord of Darkness. No other would ever steal her heart as he had done.

The man who silently entered the solar behind her was tall and powerfully built, dressed casually in hide breeches and a long shirt, open to the waist, revealing a muscular chest dark with hair. He possessed a hard face, with deep lines etched each side of the lean mouth, but both softened as he stood listening to the soft words being spoken to the child at the woman's breast, watching with pale glittering green eyes the long fingers which stroked the curly head. There were times when they were as cold as ice, but at this moment they contained the warmth of the sun in which he stood, drinking in the beauty of the scene.

Without a sound he crossed the room and relaxed easily down on to the sofa facing Alisandre. She never ceased to wonder at the stealth with which he could move. Like her shadow, he was always with her, she thought, as she lifted her head to smile at him.

'Are you not practising at the quintain this afternoon, my love?' she asked softly, secretly pleased by his early arrival.

'And miss these moments with you?' Rollo's low tones sent a thrill of excitement through her, as did the gleam which sprang to his eyes. He had something other in mind than watching her feed his son, she knew. 'I have practised enough these past days. Tomorrow we leave for the coast, and I would not waste these last hours in the company of my men.

They are well trained, and glad that I am leaving them in peace,' he added with a chuckle as he stretched long legs out in front of him, allowing his body to relax into the softness of the cushions.

He was a hard man to please, Alisandre knew that full well, but the demands he made upon the men who fought for him were never questioned. It was an honour to be part of the Guard of the Lord of Darkness—the name given to those he selected to be his personal retinue, who never numbered more than six at any time. Men would have sold their souls to be that close to this legendary knight whose exploits on the battlefield were told and retold whenever soldiers gathered together, but Rollo did not want their souls. He demanded their loyalty, the utmost skill with sword and battleaxe and even bare hands. Alertness of mind, swiftness of foot—everything that kept a man alive in battle—and afterwards.

'I think I am jealous of my son,' Rollo remarked, folding his arms across his broad chest. 'I want to spend time with you, and you neglect me for your son.'

'Our son,' she retorted swiftly, knowing he did not mean the words, although there were times when his jealousy had given her cause for disquiet, and probably would in the future. If another man so much as cast a look at her, Rollo's black temper was provoked. 'Do not say such things to me!'

'Then call Berta, and let her put the child to bed. See, he is asleep. And I would be where he is now,' he added, wicked lights springing to the eyes that watched her.

'Rollo, you are impossible!' Alisandre whispered, colour slowly rising in her cheeks.

'You did not say that yesterday—or the day before, when we stopped to rest the horses. I want you now, Kutti. You have satisifed Jarl, will you not do the same for me?'

'I shall take him to the nursery and return immediately.'

'Nay, I shall take him, or you will be gossiping with Berta until nightfall.' Lithe as a mountain cat, Rollo sprang to his feet and took the sleeping infant from her. Strong hands held him against his chest and for a moment Alisandre watched amusedly as he gazed down into the sleeping face. 'He will be handsome, this son of ours. Not too handsome, I hope, or he will be the plague of some father's life before he is of age. How the girls will love him!'

'Are you thinking of our son's future—or your own past?' Alisandre laughed softly. 'I seem to remember you were fond of the ladies yourself, when you were young.'

'And now I have the ill fortune to love just one, who starves me of affection and reminds me of past indiscretions!' Rollo grinned.

'You shall have the chance to make amends for those harsh words in a moment.'

Alisandre rose to her feet when she was alone, stretching cramped limbs, her eyes thoughtful as she was drawn to the window by the sounds from below.

The courtyard was a hive of activity. The smith was busy ensuring that the horses and pack-mules were in condition to make the journey to the coast, where they were to meet King Richard and Queen Berengaria and take a ship for Cyprus and, from there, another to France. Overland after that to the court of Richard's mother, the Dowager Queen Eleanor, where they would remain and rest for a while before making the final sea crossing to England.

She sighed, drinking in the scenes below that she knew she might not see again for many months, perhaps for years. They would have to sustain her through whatever lay ahead. How she wished her memory had returned before she started out for her old home, but it was painfully slow in returning. All recollections of her past life, obliterated on that day in Jerusalem when it had fallen to the Saracens, had not completely returned. Sometimes the slowness of her recovery made her feel confused, incomplete as a person. She had been assured by the learned doctors who had examined her that one day her memory would come back. Soon, she prayed . . . Soon. I must know everything.

Her attention was focused on the men directly below. One man, tall, with a scarred face, wore the white, black and silver livery of the Lord of Darkness, as did his companions. Siward, the Norseman, was Rollo's right hand, and friend. Hers, too, now, although there had been a time when he had wanted to kill her. Chavo, the young tousle-headed squire, had been given the important task of remaining behind at Shah'mat, keeping it secure until his lord returned. He had fallen in love with Céline, Alisandre's Arab maid, and she, too, would be remaining behind. One-armed Guyon still fought with the skill and courage of a man with two arms; his remaining fingers had pinched many a bottom, including that of Berta, Jarl's nurse.

The closing of the door brought her about. Rollo returned to the sofa and reclined there, demanding, when she did not move, 'Do I have to wait all day, Kutti?'

Alisandre stretched languidly, lifting her arms above her head like a cat awakening from a deep sleep—indeed, was that not what his pet name for her meant?—aware of his narrowed eyes following the upward rise of her breasts where the gown still gaped across her golden skin.

'Do I have to come and fetch you, woman?' he growled impatiently, and she relented and went to him and was immediately seized in a fierce grip. Searing kisses parted her mouth. His hands pushed away the bodice of her gown still further to free her breasts, cup the softness of them, trail his lips from hers, to her neck, to the pale pink nipples already hard with desire beneath his probing fingers.

'Rollo, you are so impatient... What if someone should come in?' Alisandre whispered, not really caring any more if they were interrupted. He always did this to her. The moment she felt his touch against her bare skin or his lips on hers, she had no will of her own.

'I have given instructions that we are not to be disturbed,' he murmured, lifting his lips to the mane of tawny gold hair which was spread across the cushions. 'I want to remember this last time, here in Shah'mat. It will be a very special memory.'

'Am I to sleep alone tonight, then?' Alisandre teased, locking her hands behind his neck, caressing the thick black curls at its base.

'Witch! You shall not leave my side one instant until the morning.' He looked down into the bright blue eyes intent on his face. Blue like the summer sky, like the sea, yet possessing a hint of green in their depths. Her lips parted expectantly as he undressed her without haste, stroking, kissing, teasing her as she had teased him. As he drew back to divest himself of his own unwanted clothing, he caught his breath at the perfection of the body waiting to receive him.

Whereas his own was sun-bronzed, hardened by years of fighting, scarred on the back and one leg, and on his shoulders, hers was soft, with golden sun-kissed skin, the stomach flat and smooth even after the birth of their son. Her breasts fuller now, perfectly rounded, the secret place between those long legs, where only he had ever dared to venture, enticing him down over her.

'Rollo.' The whispered name was lost beneath the fierce pressure of his mouth on hers, as his weight pressed her further into the cushions.

He parted her thighs and sank deep into her, his hands never still, his lips following those of his son's to the rosebud nipples. This would be the last night they made love at Shah'mat, but Alisandre closed her mind to the fact, abandoning herself instead to the fire beginning to consume her, the sheer delight of the sensations running up and down her spine, the heightening of her senses, drawing her closer and closer to the culmination of their lovemaking.

Rollo's slow movements inside her prolonged her desire for that final joining as one, and her long nails sank into the scarred shoulders as her hips arched upwards, betraying her need to him. She heard him chuckle in her ear and the whispered words, 'Now who grows impatient, Kutti?' as his thrusting quickened.

The sun had gone completely from the solar, and shadows lengthened about the room. The parrot still dozed, uninterrupted by the sounds of muffled laughter, of whispered endearments and muted cries of passion which came from the sofa. The infiltration of dusk upon the scene discreetly enveloped the lovers in a cloak of modesty, for which Céline was glad as she opened the door and peered cautiously inside. She had knocked twice, loudly, but no one had answered and she had thought them perhaps to be asleep—until a voice declared curtly out of the gathering darkness,

'What the devil do you want, girl?'

'Hush, my love,' her mistress murmured, and then there was a moment's silence.

Céline suspected a kiss was being given to compensate for the inopportune arrival. Allah be thankful that her mistress always knew how to handle this unpredictable man! Even in his blackest mood, he could be placated by the woman who had stolen his heart.

'It is growing late, we must not linger. Later...'

'What is it?' This time Rollo's tone was less gruff and intimidating.

'Siward needs you below, my lord. To inspect the pack train.'

'Damnation, the man is capable of doing that for himself!'

'He was most insistent, my lord.'

'We shall both go down,' Alisandre murmured, and there was a blur of white as two bodies came reluctantly apart, a rustling of silk as she slipped on her gown, a muttering as Rollo pulled on his own clothes. 'I promise I shall not leave your side for an instant... Tell Siward we shall join him immediately, Céline.'

'One more minute alone,' Rollo insisted, as she lighted one of the oil-lamps suspended from the ceiling and stood framed in the glow which highlighted the flame strands of hair falling about her bare shoulders. He came to her and laid his hands gently upon her shoulders.

She turned her head to press her lips against his hand. 'Rollo...' She was hesitant to speak of it, to bring back the pain. 'I know we must go, but I feel as if I am being torn in two. I am leaving so much of me behind. Help me!'

His arms went about her, drawing her against his chest, and she buried her face against his shirt, her eyes growing moist as she thought of those four years whose memory was denied her. The only three people she loved in all the world had been taken from her. But God had been generous. Some of her shattered memory had returned, and he had bestowed on her even a more wonderful gift—the love of the Lord of Darkness. Such a love would not be found again in her lifetime. They had come to each other in the midst of war and treachery, had survived intrigue and deception. Trust had replaced suspicion; love, pain and loneliness. A true miracle!

'I shall always be at your side, Kutti. Always, I swear it.' It cut Rollo deeply to see her suffering. 'Nothing will ever change between us. I will not let it.'

He kissed her slowly, lingering for that one last moment before they left the room, and she, comforted by the deep, vibrant passion in his voice, allowed him to lead her out of the solar.

When the ship bringing them from Calais put them ashore at a small village on the Solent, heavy black clouds in the sky had greeted their arrival, followed by a storm and high winds which soaked them to the skin as they made their way to the shelter of a nearby monastery. The suspicious, unsmiling faces that peered at them from the windows of dirty-looking hovels with tightly closed doors were as ungracious and as unwelcoming as the weather.

Mid-December was not a good time to cross the English Channel, and as Rollo remembered the warmth of Palestine, the comfort of Shah'mat and the brilliantly sunny days, he scowled to himself and drew his cloak more tightly about his body. He was cold, and it was not just from the rain and the miserable weather, he knew, for his face ran with sweat. It was the old sickness he had contracted while a prisoner of the Saracens. He might last another few hours in the saddle, but not much longer.

They could reach Wynterfold in another day if they rode continuously, but by then the fever would be raging through his body and he might well have lost all sense of reason, as had happened before. He silently cursed the malady that afflicted him. It would cost him precious time and delay the many plans he had made. He was anxious to settle the matter of Alisandre's estate, situated not far from the city of Winchester. Once she was installed there as the rightful mistress, he intended to return to France again. He glanced at the woman riding beside him. Her beauty was all but obscured by the heavy cloak shrouding her from head to toe; only her pale face showed beneath the fur-trimmed cowl. The face that was with him in his dreams at night, as well as every waking moment. They had become as one, inseparable. If he should ever lose her...

Tomorrow, Winchester, then to London to discover if the Dowager Queen's fears of John's treachery were true or false. To discover also why the people of England did not rejoice for the return of their lawful king. Richard had sailed from Acre two months before, but his ship had become separated from the fleet in a storm and carried north to the island of Corfu. Now December was upon them and not one person Rollo had conversed with knew anything about the return of Richard Coeur-de-Lion. Had he come incognito, seeking to discover for himself if his brother's lust for power and riches was more than rumour, more than anxious letters written to him by ministers whose authority had been usurped? Why had he not gone to his mother's court at Poitiers, if he were safe and well? She would tell him everything he needed to know.

In England, the people waited for the return of their king, and England was now where Alisandre found herself on this cold, unfriendly day. She had not wanted to come here, but now she was aware of a growing excitement within her which she could no longer ignore. Wynterfold had once been her home, after all—and this was her country. She must give herself a little time to adjust.

Rollo's mailed hand closed tightly round the pommel of his saddle as a wave of dizziness swept over him, and he felt himself reel unsteadily.

'You are not well, my love. We must find somewhere to stay for the night. You cannot sleep out in the open any more. I fear you have caught a chill,' Alisandre said softly, her keen eyes not missing the movement. 'Wynterfold can wait another few days for me.'

Rollo smiled faintly. 'You are not as anxious to see your old home again as I thought you would be.'

'That is because I find it hard to think of England as my home any longer,' Alisandre returned. 'I have been away seven years. I do not feel the same about

Wynterfold as you do about your French home,
Verduse. I thought the place held too many bitter
memories for you to ever think of rebuilding it again,
let alone living there.'

She had watched him wander around the ruined
castle set between the rolling green hills of Provence
with a river close by, seen him pause for a long
moment over the grave of his dead wife, the woman
who had betrayed him during their marriage and
poisoned his heart and soul against ever loving again.
He had vowed never to return there, that once
Alisandre had established her rights as mistress of
Wynterfold, they would return to Palestine with their
son and shut themselves away in the fortress of
Shah'mat, away from the world and the fighting and
the mistrust that man harboured for his fellow man.
He had promised! Yet the day before they left the
Dowager Queen's court, he had astounded Alisandre
by announcing that he intended to use some of the
wealth he had brought back with him to restore
Verduse. She naturally assumed that that was where
he intended them to live for the rest of their lives.

'Our son must have his natural inheritance. I cannot
deny him his rights. Next Christmas we shall not be
in this miserable, rain-sodden land where we are regarded as intruders, but where we belong. You and
I—and Jarl—as it should be.' He broke off, reeling
in the saddle, and Alisandre gave a cry.

'Gy should have been back by now.' She was referring to Rollo's squire, whom he had sent ahead at

least an hour before to seek shelter for the night. 'Should you not send someone after him?'

'All he has to contend with in this forest are wild animals, not armed Saracens!' Rollo gave a tight smile.

'Will you not ride in the litter for a while, then?' she pleaded.

'When I fall unconscious from my horse, you can bundle me into the litter,' he told her with an accompanying look that was contemptuous of the suggestion. His fierce Norman pride forbade him to show any weakness before the men who rode watchfully behind him—Siward, the Norseman, Cerdic, Gerhard and Guyon.

'Gy comes, my lord.' Siward kneed his horse forward to join Rollo, pointing ahead to the path that twisted away from them into dense undergrowth. 'And riding as if the devil were after his soul!'

'If he has no good explanation for his long absence, he will have more than the devil to contend with,' Rollo growled.

Alisandre smiled to herself on hearing the stern tone.

'Well?' Rollo demanded as a young boy in his late teens reined in before them. 'What was her name?'

'My lord, you do me a great wrong,' Gy Savennes gasped, ignoring Siward, who raised a speculative eyebrow and waited for the tale of fantasy to begin. If Gy did not become a knight, he would become the best teller of tales in the world. 'What people I have seen ran from me. They barricaded the doors of the hovels they call homes and would not come out.'

'Afraid of you—a mere stripling?' Behind them, Guyon snorted in disbelief, but Rollo's frown silenced further comment.

'I found but three dwellings, my lord, and none of them worth a look from you, certainly not fit for you and the Lady Alisandre to rest overnight. From the murderous looks I got, I'd say we'd all end up with daggers in our backs, stripped of our clothes and left in the forest. It was eerie to ride through the trees and see so few signs of life. I thought to find a pig or a few fat chickens so that we could at least eat well to-night, but even the animals are scarce. I saw two scrawny chickens which Siward could down in one mouthful, and a pig so small... I swear it is the truth,' he added, flushing as Rollo's gaze narrowed and sparks of anger flickered in the depths of the pale green eyes.

'The peasants here can be no different from any others—they must have rights from their lord. From September until November their animals have been able to graze on the acorns hereabouts. Look at the oak trees, boy, and tell me that there is not enough food to fatten a few pigs?'

'I have found a place, my lord, with a cripple and a girl. They have only one room, but there is a barn of sorts. Come and see for yourself that I speak the truth.'

'If he does not, I will find an apple and stop up his mouth once and for all!' Siward threatened. 'Lead on, boy. I suppose you can find it again?'

'You are too hard on him, both of you,' Alisandre said, as Gy turned his horse about and began to lead the way. 'He speaks only a few Saxon words and probably could not make himself understood.'

'Or it is true that John is taxing the people of this country out of their very livelihood?' Rollo murmured. 'The only hospitality we have been shown came from the monks who gave us shelter, learned men who knew where we came from and what we have been doing these past years. These others regard us as intruders.'

'And their table was not lacking in food,' his wife reminded him. 'When we reach Wynterfold, I am sure you will be shown good Saxon hospitality. I shall make sure of it.'

'The church always fares better than anyone else,' came the dry reply. 'Their coffers will still be full, along with their stomachs, while others, less fortunate, starve.'

As a precaution, Rollo ordered two of his Guard to drop back and ride behind the litter. He sensed disquiet in the forest, and despite the illness now rapidly numbing his senses, he knew there was danger about. In what shape or form it would come he did not know, but at least they would be prepared.

Eventually, Gy reined in his horse and pointed ahead. Alisandre's eyes widened at the sight of the place before them, little more than a mud hovel, with wooden supports for the one ill-shaped window. A hole in the roof served as a chimney, and from this issued a stream of greyish black smoke into the snow-laden sky. A young woman was gathering up twigs from a pile on the ground outside the door. At the sight of them, she disappeared inside, dropping the bundle in her haste.

'Show yourselves. We mean you no harm.' Rollo's commanding tones rang about the small clearing.

After a moment a man appeared, limping heavily as he stepped from the hut and took several hesitant steps in their direction. His clothes were little more than rags, his beard and hair, worn long as was the Saxon style, were matted and unkempt.

'Lord, we have nothing. Your men took the last of our livestock only yesterday. . .' The quavering voice was full of fear, and Alisandre laid a hand upon her husband's arm as he opened his mouth to speak again.

'We need shelter for the night. That is all we ask. Since when have Saxons turned strangers from their doors, denying them even the barest of courtesies?'

'We have no room here, lady. Not for the likes of you—and your friends.' The man's tone was hostile, despite the obvious disability which meant he could not ably defend himself against any attack.

Before he had finished speaking, Siward had leaped from his horse to confront him, his hand on his sword. As he did so, the Guard moved forward protectively to flank their lord and his lady, each one of them angered that this peasant dared to speak to them in such a manner. Did these Englishmen not know their place?

'Do not speak to the Lady Alisandre again like that—or I will have your tongue!' Siward threatened.

'Take it! You have taken everything else for your precious master.' The reply was so startling that it froze them all, set minds racing as to what was happening in this land since Richard had departed its shores.

'Siward—no! Do not touch him. Can you not see there is little enough here for him, let alone for us? All we ask is a dry place to sleep tonight,' Alisandre appealed to the young woman who peered cautiously over the man's shoulder. Young? She could have been twenty, or twice that age. Heavy lines etched a perhaps once pretty face. Her body beneath the ill-fitting dress of drab brown was pathetically thin, her hair as unkempt as that of the man. They had not eaten well in a long time, she thought.

'My father does not lie, my lady. We have but one room, and the lean-to byre yonder, but the roof leaks. We have no need to repair it, for the king's men have taken all our livestock.'

'Speak you so of King Richard?' Rollo demanded.

'Nay, lord, the king—John,' she replied, looking at him as if he were slightly addled in the head. 'John is king of England now, and has been for three years past.'

'Not while Richard lives!'

Alisandre's fingers closed about Rollo's arm. He was in no condition to worry himself about the strangeness of the woman's words. 'Within the hour, your roof will be repaired,' she said confidently. 'We shall stay. Gy, you will find wood for a fire. Take another man with you. Siward, help my husband. You others attend to the roof. I must prepare a broth of meat and herbs as quickly as possible.' As once before, when Rollo had been stricken down with the same malady and had lain feverish and helpless in the desert, she took charge of the situation.

Rollo stifled a groan as he dismounted, and reluctantly accepted the arm Siward offered. His legs trembled and barely kept him upright. His head was swimming, his vision blurred. 'Get me to shelter,' he said in a harsh whisper. 'Out of sight of these gaping wretches.' He lurched, rather than walked, the few steps to the lean-to beside the hut, desperately fighting the swirling blackness that threatened to drag him down into the realms of unconsciousness and the hell which followed.

For a moment, as she stepped over the threshold into the hut, Alisandre was transported back to the dungeon in Acre where Rollo had found her, the nauseous smell of animal excreta and rotting straw invading her nostrils. In the fading light coming through the holes in the wattle roof, she could almost imagine the cheeky beggar-boy, Omar, kneeling in the shadows watching her, trying to make her accept who and what she was before the Crusaders stormed the city and liberated the many Christian prisoners in the cells.

Taking a bundle of furs and bedding from Cerdic's arms, she sent him to help the other man repairing the roof, and quickly prepared a makeshift bed on the uneven floor. She frowned as she helped Siward to lower Rollo on to it, and felt how his skin burned beneath her touch. Gently she bent and laid her lips against his, whispering softly, 'Rest, my love. By morning you will be stronger.' But as she straightened and climbed to her feet, her eyes told Siward a different story, and he followed her outside in silence. 'We shall be here a day at least. I think for longer, and then he will be too weak to sit a horse. You remember how it was the last time? Whether he likes it or not, he is going to be carried the rest of the way to Wynterfold.'

'He will not like it,' Siward said with a dry smile, 'but you are right. There is not enough room in the litter for him and Berta and the child. We need a cart. I will find one tomorrow, and we shall leave here as soon as you think he can be moved. I do not feel easy here with these peasants.'

'Take money, and pay for it, Siward. The people hereabouts seem to have little enough. I will not steal what I want from them, as others are doing. The king has returned to an unhappy land.'

'Why did the woman speak of John as the king? Richard is alive and well—and home again!'

'I have no answer—nor time to think of one. Please stay with my husband until I have fed my son.'

Alisandre found Berta crouching terrified at the back of the covered litter, with Jarl in her arms, only his little face, bright red from crying, visible against her large bosom. She had plucked up enough courage to poke her head outside once after they had stopped, and quickly withdrawn it at the sight of their unfriendly surroundings, and the two dirty peasants who offered them not a glimmer of a smile on their grimy faces, let alone an offer of hospitality. Not that she wanted to spend a night beneath that roof, to be eaten alive by bugs and whatever else infested it!

'Mistress, we are not staying here!' she declared in horror. 'We shall all be murdered as we sleep by those—those . . .'

'By a half-starved man and his daughter? Alisandre said, her tone scornful. 'They are more afraid of us than we are of them, believe me. Guyon shall sleep beneath the wagon tonight, so you will be quite safe.'

'With him! He may have only one arm, but my bottom is black and blue when he is about! Besides, where will you be? Not—in there?'

'My lord is ill, and he needs me. I shall stay with him. Now give me Jarl and make yourself useful. I shall need my pouch of herbs and powders. Find it, and take it to Siward, then go to the supply wagon and find some meat. I think there is some salted beef left, and vegetables. Ask the woman for a large cooking-pot to make a broth. We shall all have need of something hot and nourishing before this night is over.'

Alisandre removed her cloak and loosened her bodice so that she could put Jarl to her breast. As he began to suckle hungrily, she relaxed and held him more tightly. He still had a healthy appetite, but at nine months he was not as big as he should have been, in her estimation. The long journey from Palestine and across Europe to England had taken the colour from his cheeks, and he had been denied familiar faces and toys that had become important to him. She ran her fingers through the mass of tiny red curls flecked with gold—her hair, his father's eyes. A striking combination. Placated by the warmth of his mother's softness against him, and well fed, Jarl fell into a deep sleep and was easily relinquished once more into Berta's arms.

'Gy has a good fire going, mistress, and the young rascal found two hares, caught in traps. They're skinned and in the pot. The woman has a few beans and berries, which she says they eat all the time. I left those for you to see. Mayhap she's trying to poison us!'

'And sign her own death-warrant? I doubt if she's that much of a fool. How is my husband?' Alisandre pulled on her cloak, covering her two thick braids of fiery tresses with the cowl.

'The Norseman is with him; he would not let me near him. As if he knows what to do for a sick man!' To Berta, only one person was allowed to be protective about Rollo and Alisandre, and that was herself. 'Get you to your lord. He has greater need of you.'

Alisandre climbed from the litter, drawing her cloak close about her, as a chill night wind threatened to

tear it from her back. She could just make out the
abundance of brush and undergrowth that had been
cut and lain on the top of the roof, covering every
hole. Torches had been fashioned and placed beside
the lean-to, lighting up the area in front of it. Siward,
she thought gratefully. If danger did lurk in the forest,
they would not be taken unawares, for no one could
now approach without being seen. The man and his
daughter were nowhere about, but a faint glow came
from inside their hut.

Over an enormous fire, which she knew would be
kept alight for the remainder of the night, squatted
Gy, poking with a long wooden spoon at the cauldron
suspended over it on a rusty iron tripod. A few feet
away, Cerdic and Gerhard sat cleaning their swords.
Guyon would be tending to the horses, she suspected,
because that kept him close to Berta, to whom he had
taken rather a fancy over the past months. Despite
her scorn of his wandering hand, the attraction was
mutual.

Siward began to rise to his feet as she entered, but
she motioned him to stay seated. As she slipped to
her knees beside her husband, his eyes opened and
his hand sought hers, the fingers tightening over her
own quite painfully.

'Once again, I am in your hands, Kutti.' Like most
soldiers, he disliked, even feared, being helpless. She
saw that his sword and axe had been placed close
beside him. She doubted if he had the strength to lift
either at the moment, but her heart swelled with love
and pride to think he would try, if it became necessary.

'Don't talk, my love. Sleep. I am here, and your Guard protect us all. Who is there to best them? Tomorrow, the worst will be over. I am here beside you. I love you, Rollo, my husband, my Lord of Darkness. Sleep.'

An hour later, she sat back on her heels and gave a soft sigh. 'He sleeps, but we must watch him closely through the night to ensure that he is always warm, or the fever could last for days.'

Carefully, so as not to disturb him, she uncurled Rollo's fingers. After he had taken the bowl of broth containing the medicinal powders that would alleviate the malady, he had clung to her, saying nothing, but watching her as she sat beside him. She wondered if his thoughts were of the past, or if it was his way of holding on to reality until his mind began to wander, as she knew it would within a few hours, before the fever left his body and his strength began to return.

'Everyone has eaten?' asked Alisandre, stretching her cramped limbs.

'Everyone except you. Let me bring you something.'

'I am not hungry.'

She smiled faintly into the scarred face, grateful not only for his concern, but his company. Siward was the only one of the Guard to whom Rollo allowed such familiarity, but he trusted the Norseman implicitly, as she did. She wandered to the door, and pushed aside the cloth that someone had draped there to keep out the cold. Gy dozed beside the fire. Gerhard and Cerdic stood watchfully on either side of him.

No rest for them tonight. Light still flickered in the peasants' hut. Impulsively she approached the fire and shook the young squire into wakefulness.

'Gy, fill two bowls with stew, with plenty of meat, and follow me,' she ordered. Most Saxons still retained a deep-rooted dislike of their Norman overlords, she suspected. She would show them that they had nothing to fear from the Duke of Aquitaine.

'My lady?' The boy blinked up at her stupidly, then scrambled to his feet and did as he was bid.

'Come.'

Gy stumbled after her to the door of the hut, not yet fully awake, but somehow managing not to spill any liquid from the two silver bowls he carried.

'Greetings! I have brought you some food.' Alisandre heard a movement from inside, whispers, and then silence again. Her lips pursed in annoyance, she stepped over the threshold into the half light which came from a fire smouldering in the centre of the floor. In the rainy season, the place would be ankle-deep in mud, she realised. The man and woman stood to one side of her, the latter's hand tightly clutching her father's arm. A bed of bracken, covered with something that resembled an animal hide, was behind them. The only other piece of furniture was a small table.

The curling smoke blinded her, and she lifted a ringed hand to wave it away from her face, aware of two pairs of eyes staring at the magnificent ruby on her little finger.

'Give them the food, Gy,' she said quietly. 'It is hot, nourishing stew made from some hares that my husband's squire found in the forest,' she assured them, as neither made a move to take the bowls held out to them. They stared wide-eyed at the delicate silverwork and the engraved coat of arms. It was obvious that neither had seen anything like them before. 'Put them down and let us go. We cannot make them eat,' she added with a shrug.

It was as she was turning to follow the squire out that a faint movement from the far side of the fire caught her eye. At first she thought it to be a dog, although she had not seen one show itself. She blinked to clear her eyes, and felt the icy fingers of fear reach out and touch her. Not a dog, but a man clad in dark clothing that had enabled him to blend into the shadows and not be seen. Another movement froze her where she stood, for she knew that what he held in his hands was a crossbow, and the bolt in it was aimed at her heart.

CHAPTER TWO

'Is YOUR friend not also hungry?' Alisandre asked in a quiet voice, which she somehow managed to keep steady despite the wild pounding of her heart.

'You have keen eyes, lady.' The slowly-spoken words, the weapon which continued to be pointed at her heart, told her this man was not like the other two occupants of the hut. He was someone to be reckoned with—an unknown quantity. At any moment he could loose the bolt and end her life. He knew of the men outside, yet he menaced her, quite prepared to kill her. A poacher? Few peasants possessed such weapons, she reasoned. An outlaw? The forest was a perfect hiding-place for such men, with food in abundance if they did not mind killing the king's deer— and if a man was outside the law, that was a triviality. Why was she not afraid of him? Yet why should she be? She had faced Rollo's anger, distrust and hatred— and still she lived. After *his* wrath, no man could ever frighten her!

But she was afraid *for* him, lying defenceless in the byre yonder. Siward and the Guard would protect him with their lives, but if there were more like this one, secreted about the place...

'There is food outside if you are not afraid to show your face, messire. I know not who you are, and I care not. My husband and I have sought shelter here because he is ill, but do not think we are helpless. The men with him are recently returned from the Holy Land. They are soldiers—and loyal to us. They will not allow us to be robbed and killed by some forest outlaw!'

A soft chuckle came out of the shadows and curling smoke which divided them. Through the haze, she saw that the crossbow was lowered.

'You are no Norman! Is it possible that you have a little Saxon blood in you, lady?'

'I am the Lady Alisandre de Greville-Wynter, returning to my home of Wynterfold.' Why she had deigned to give him her name was beyond her, yet some instinct told her that they had not stumbled on some ordinary peasant's hut. Not with this man here! 'My father's blood-line was mingled with that of Saxon kings long before England ever knew what a Norman looked like. And in those days men were not afraid to show their faces! Use your weapon, or save that bolt for some animal in the forest tomorrow by which you will live another day. I have more important things to do than stand here and talk with you while my husband lies ill.'

'Your Norman husband! Another of Count John's lackeys?'

'My husband is lackey to no man! He is Rollo, Duke of Aquitaine, who these past years has been fighting at the side of King Richard himself, a man he calls friend. Ally—yes! Honourable knight—yes! Lackey—no!'

Alisandre turned on her heel, pulling her cloak tightly about her as she stepped outside again. She knew she was well within range of the crossbow as she neared the byre, ducked and entered, and stood trembling, her cheeks ashen.

Siward turned to stare at her, and then took two quick steps to her side, his hands resting, oh, so carefully, on her shoulders. 'My lady, you look ill! Come by the fire, warm yourself. What were you doing outside?'

She allowed herself to be drawn to the fire, her cloak to be removed by impersonal hands. He brought her wine, heated over the fire and infused with herbs. She sipped gratefully, using the few moments of silence which passed between them to contain herself again. She explained how she had gone to the peasants' hut to offer them food, and told of the man in the shadows who had menaced her. The words were hardly out of her mouth before Siward was on his feet, his hand on his sword.

'No, stay.' Her hand on his arm detained him as he turned towards the entrance. 'I do not believe he is a threat to us, whoever he is.'

'A man holding a crossbow with a bolt aimed at your heart *is* a threat, my lady, believe me!' came the grim answer.

'Then why did he not kill me? He knew I would come back here and tell someone of his presence. He is no friend of the king's brother, from his tone of voice. Such hatred when he spoke the name—contempt for anyone who might serve John. The country has fared ill while King Richard has been away.'

'Then why have we seen no signs of rejoicing at his return? The land lies dead, one large graveyard, and as for the people...' Siward shook his head in puzzlement. 'I am of a mind to seek out this man and shake some answers from him.'

'There's no need for that. He's come to speak with you, as bold as you please. He demanded to be brought into the presence of the Saxon lady. Did I do right to bring him to you, Lady Alisandre?' Cerdic stood in the entrance, his dagger at the throat of a tall, thin man. 'He's unarmed. I searched him well,' he added, as Siward moved protectingly to shield Alisandre with his own body.

'Yes, Cerdic. Leave us, but stay close while we question him,' she ordered.

'Send Guyon to the peasants' hut. He'll find a crossbow there. With Lord Rollo unable to protect you himself, my lady, that duty is mine,' Siward told her as she opened her mouth to protest, and she nodded acquiescence.

Now that she could see the stranger's features clearly, she noted that he bore a close resemblance to the other two Saxons, but his bearing was different, and the gaze which considered them both was un-afraid—almost mocking. Her heart missed a beat. Did he have men hidden near by after all, to fall on them, kill them and steal the many valuables they had with them? His grey hair was cut shorter and was less un-kempt, the beard quite presentable, as were the plain homespun clothes. Once a man of substance, was the impression that came into her mind. What was he doing hiding in the forest in a peasant's filthy hut?

'We are at a disadvantage. You know who we are,' she said with quiet dignity as she seated herself beside her husband and briefly touched his hand to reassure herself that his fever had not worsened.

'My name is Will Appleton, the finest fletcher Wynterfold has ever seen. You would not remember me, my lady, I don't expect, but I once worked for your father. And after him—when it was known that he and your sainted mother had perished in Jerusalem and you along with them—for that devil Hugo de Greville-Wynter, your cousin. May he roast in hell!'

'You are right, I don't remember you. I was only a young girl when I left Wynterfold,' Alisandre replied slowly, searching her memory for some place where this face would fit, but she found none. 'How do you know that my cousin is dead?'

'The news was brought to his sister, the Lady Margaret, by one Roger Chabret, a knight who fought at his side,' came the instant reply.

If he was lying, he was well versed, she thought.

'Most likely one of those who tried to stab our lord in the back that day,' Siward growled, reminding her of the tournament when Rollo had fought Hugo de Greville-Wynter. The winner decreed whether she herself lived or died. For a moment she was transported back to the heat and the dust of the combat, the wild cries of the onlookers, the mêlée which almost resulted in Rollo's death through the treachery of Hugo's followers.

'Since the king departed for the Crusade, there have been oppressive taxes which have bled the people dry. They have no money, and little food on which to live. And did you know that Count John proclaimed himself—not Arthur of Brittany, whom King Richard named as his successor—to assume the throne if anything happened to his brother?'

'I did not. Neither did any of us. Tell us some of these wrongs you say have been perpetrated, Will Appleton, and be sure to speak only the truth. Your life depends on it!' Siward growled.

The man cast an almost amused look in Siward's direction. He was not afraid of death; threats would not induce him to talk. He had come to them of his own free will. Why? Alisandre wondered. Was it because she had mentioned that Rollo was not only a Crusader knight, but a friend and ally of King Richard? In the hut, she had sensed she faced an enemy, but now his attitude had changed and she needed to know why.

'When King Richard left England, he took with him all the men he could bribe, force or coerce into his service,' Will said, ignoring the black look directed by the Norseman. 'I am a Saxon. I see no reason why I should fight for a Norman king who spends his time out of the country he is supposed to be protecting. We were better under our own kind! But that has nothing to do with what I tell you now. Even while Richard was on his way to Acre, Longchamp, the very man he had left in control, took an oath of fealty to Count John, acknowledging *him* as heir to the throne.'

'How could such a thing happen?' Alisandre breathed. 'Who dared to support such treason?'

'The Count—or Prince John as he likes to be known—is a clever, devious man, my lady. He has a winning way about him, when bribes and land-grants do not work. Longchamp had no choice in the matter. He had become too thirsty for power. Some say the taxes he extracted from the people never reached the king but went into his own pocket. How else could he travel the countryside with the retinue he had? Why, to look on him was like looking on the king himself, so splendid were the trappings of his horse and livery, his men at arms. He, not the king, ruled England, and John took advantage of that fact to turn the people against him. To take power from his hands.'

'Power given to him by King Richard,' Siward interrupted. 'How was that possible? The barons should never have permitted it. From all I hear, they are no friend of the king's brother.'

'Not many, I admit, but there are always those who wish to further their ambitious schemes, to fill their coffers with more gold and silver by siding with whoever offers them the best terms. As I've told you, John is no fool.'

'Nor are you, Will Appleton,' Alisandre remarked quietly, and a pair of beady brown eyes rested thoughtfully on the slender figure sitting beside the unconscious man, who was clad in a halberk and over-tunic of black, with a distinctive emblem em-

broidered on it—a bolt of lightning split asunder. He
had never seen the like of it before. A bold insignia.
A man to go against the usurper of the king's throne,
perhaps? But he was a Norman! All Normans were
the same. 'Please continue. How did the king's
brother gain so much power?'

'I was in London the day it happened, my lady.
The whole city was awakened by the tocsin, the bell
that rings if danger threatens. People poured into the
streets in their hundreds, and found heralds in the
streets, proclaiming a great meeting of the most important men in the land at St Paul's Church. At first
we thought the king was dead. What else could have
aroused such men of prominence to leave their comfortable homes and their women to assemble in the
city? So everyone went to St Paul's, myself among
them. Everyone was there—all the barons, the most
influential men in the land—and Count John. Few
understand what was said to us for it was in their own
tongue, a mixture of French and Norman with a few
Saxon words thrown in to appease us, I suspect, when
they thought we should understand something they
wanted. Yet their manner was different. For so many
years we Saxons have been treated lower than offal!
Yet that day we were shown—at a distance, of course,
and even though I pushed my way to the front of the
crowd, all I could see was a seal, and official though
it looked, I did not believe it—a letter from King
Richard, depriving Longchamp of his office should
he fail in his duty. The barons and bishops and earls
voted that he had not carried out his duties and that

he should be deprived of his chancellorship, and that John, the king's brother, should assume full powers. The Chancellor was in the Tower, hiding, they say, at the time. When he was told the news, he not only gave the keys of the Tower into John's hands, but swore an oath to surrender the keys of other royal fortresses in his charge. I have heard a rumour that he disguised himself as a pedlar-woman in order to leave these shores for Normandy. Can you imagine that! A man accustomed to travelling with a retinue of almost a thousand men at arms, in luxury and comfort! God curse him, the coward! With him gone, there is no one to oppose Prince John, the power-hungry devil!'

'I remember that the king did receive some letters in the Holy Land which greatly upset him,' Alisandre said. 'My husband told me. Perhaps if things had not been so unsettled here, Richard might have pressed on to Jerusalem. No—perhaps not. It was written that he would never set foot in the Holy City.'

Siward did not raise an eyebrow at the prophetic words, but he noticed Will Appleton's mouth deepen into a disapproving line. For all the king's great intentions, he had failed them. Jerusalem was still in Infidel hands, and access was allowed to some holy places only through their charity. It left a bad taste in the mouth to take charity from God-cursed heathens!

'So the king's brother now rules England,' Siward said. 'What of the king? Has nothing changed since his return? Why has he not taken John's head?'

'Return? When? I know nothing of the king's return. Neither does anyone in this land,' the man flung back, his eyes narrowing as he considered the two faces before him. 'What nonsense is this?'

'Guard your tongue, friend or I will cut it out!' the Norseman warned him. Alisandre held up a restraining hand, and he cut short the remainder of his angry comments.

'The king left the Holy Land over two months ago. My husband and I sailed in the same fleet. The weather was atrocious and some vessels were blown off course, but, even so...' She looked at Siward, a growing anxiety in the depths of her blue eyes. 'We lingered at the court of the Dowager Queen Eleanor, but he should have been here by now. Dear heaven, could something have happened to him?'

'I fear you may be right, my lady.' Will's tone was again more deferential. 'For a week now, perhaps more, the prince's men have been in abundance in these parts. As...'

'Speak,' she urged. 'All our lives may well depend on what you know. My husband has no love for the king's brother. Any ally of Richard's could be in danger, and as you can well see, Rollo is ill and defenceless.'

'As if he seeks men for an army to repel—an invasion!'

'He knows,' Siward growled. 'What else could it mean? He is raising an army to keep his throne.'

'His brother's throne,' she corrected, horrified. 'There will be bloodshed throughout the land.'

'My lady, there are not men enough to rally to the king. Willing though his loyal subjects are—and Saxon or no, I'd rather have Richard than John as my king—they have no weapons. Lack of food has made them weak. Villages have been razed to the ground when taxes were not paid, men outlawed for the smallest offences, if any.'

'What crime did you commit, Will Appleton?' Alisandre asked, thinking it best to know what manner of man she might have to ask for help if this terrible news proved true.

'Your cousin, Hugo de Greville-Wynter, found my wife attractive, my lady, and suggested that I might wish to come to some agreement with him. I did not, and neither did she, but he took her anyway. She killed herself the day after he used her. I tried to kill him, but I failed. I would be dead now had it not been for friends at the house. They smuggled me out, and I have lived in the forest ever since. My brother was tortured to make him tell of my whereabouts, and was left crippled by their cruelty. I brought him and his daughter to this place, and we built this—this hut. Once they were used to better things. There are many like us throughout the country. People who would rally against John.'

'But not necessarily for their king, Richard,' Alisandre said, her shock growing at the things she was being told.

'Prince John is gathering men, you say?' Siward asked, and Will Appleton nodded. 'Men to side with him against his own brother? To hold on to the land he has stolen? He is acting as though King Richard were dead.'

'No,' Alisandre breathed. 'Don't even think that!'

'Richard, dead? Liar! The king lives—England needs him.' Rollo's eyes were open wide, the sweat pouring down his face as he struggled to sit up. 'Give me my sword—let me fight! Oh God, we are surrounded!'

'He's delirious!' Alisandre cried, throwing herself down beside her husband and pushing away the sword he tried to clutch to him. 'Hush, my love. There is no one here who will harm you.' She bent and laid her cheek against his, despite Siward's warning look.

'Soft words—always you have soft words.' The sibilant hiss alarmed her, as did the hatred which flashed suddenly into his eyes. Strong fingers closed about her throat, pressing agonisingly against her windpipe. She gasped and sank over him, trying to prise his fingers away, but they were like steel. 'Soft words from an adulteress! No more, my beautiful Lisette. No more!'

Lisette! The name seared through her brain. His dead wife! 'Forgive me, my Lord!' Through reeling senses, she heard Siward's voice. A groan, and the pressure at her throat eased. She fell back into Siward's arms, gazing down at Rollo's unconscious form. 'I had to hit him, my lady. He was mad enough to kill you. The devil curse that woman! Even now, she is in his thoughts.'

'Tell no one of this, I beg you.' Alisandre composed herself and wiped a tear from the corner of one eye. She had to be strong—for them both. 'He is not himself. Verduse has revived many unpleasant memories, and hatred. She will always be buried somewhere in his mind.'

'My niece has herbs that will cure the fever.' Will Appleton's voice penetrated her thoughts.

'My husband's health is all important, so bring your medicine, Will Appleton, and thank you. When he is well again, he will be told of your kindness.'

'A small thing—for a king's man.'

The words momentarily stunned her. Will Appleton had told them in that simple sentence where his allegiance lay.

'An honest man should not live like a hunted animal,' she said, as he turned to leave. 'If you wish, you may return to Wynterfold.'

'The Lady Margaret would roast me over an open fire! Two of a kind, she and her brother. Evil blood in both. Not that I don't trust you, my lady, but things are different at Wynterfold, as you will find out soon enough. Your cousin and Prince John are on the best of terms—if you understand my meaning. She is an ambitious woman, and he needs the men and money she raises for him. Take care. She has a devious mind, and she is cruel, but to look at her . . . I will fetch the herbs for your lord.'

Alisandre busied herself trying to make Rollo more comfortable, sponging his face with fresh rainwater from a barrel young Gy had come across outside. Had they time to linger here—two days, or three—she knew her own potions would have banished the fever lingering in his body, but she sensed danger all about them and knew they should move on as soon as possible. Siward remade the dying fire to keep them warm throughout the night. She was glad of the flames, which somehow comforted her, and the warmth, but the smoke from the wet twigs and wood made her heavy-eyed and drowsy.

'Sleep, my lady.' Siward bent over her, wrapping her cloak firmly about her. 'I will keep watch.'

'Not yet. Go and see what keeps the man...' she implored him, and he turned to leave. As he did so, the woman came to the entrance of the byre and hesitated, unsure of her welcome. In her hands she held a small wooden bowl. Alisandre took it eagerly, and at once lifted her husband's head to put the rim to his lips. He drank and coughed and tried to push it away, but she held him firmly and forced him to take the remainder. When she turned to thank the woman, she had gone.

Shouting, and the screams of a woman, followed by raucous laughter, brought Alisandre out of the realms of sleep. Rollo still slept soundly. The potion had worked a wondrous magic on him, and he had begun to grow calmer within an hour. By the time the first rays of a grey dawn began to filter through into the byre, she knew he was going to recover. It was then she had laid her head on his chest and closed her own eyes, knowing it was safe to do so.

She shivered in the keenness of the early morning air. Her mind was still fogged with sleep—was she

imagining the sounds from outside? More laughter—
screams again—and a sound that chilled her heart:
the ominous ring of steel against steel. As she came
to her feet, brushing loose strands of hair from her
eyes, Berta came running in, Jarl clutched in her arms,
and flung herself down in a corner.

'We are all going to be murdered!' she shrieked.
'Guyon, oh, Guyon, they have killed him!'

Her words sent Alisandre spinning round towards
the entrance. Heedless of the maid's warning cries
from behind, she flung aside the makeshift covering
of hides, and stepped out.

The chaotic scene that confronted her froze her
where she stood. Guyon lay face down on the ground
beside the litter, struck from behind as he protected
Berta's wild dash to the byre with Jarl. Young Gy was
held struggling and kicking by two soldiers, while
Cerdic was backed against the walls of the peasants'
hut beside the woman, Gerhard unconscious or dead
at their feet. Her father was stretched out on the
ground a few feet away beside a laughing soldier who
held a sword at his throat and looked as if he was
about to use it. Siward alone still fought the soldiers
who had come upon them while they stood around
the fire, warming cold hands and waiting for the rem-
nants of the stew in the cooking-pot to be reheated.

Twenty men against four. Well-armed, disciplined
soldiers against the Guard, who cursed the ease with
which they had been taken unawares. None of them
was afraid of death, but to be disarmed or overcome
and to have to live with the shame of knowing they

had allowed some harm to befall the man they had sworn to protect—and his lady—that was incomprehensible.

Alisandre cried out in alarm as her waist was seized by a mailed arm and she was caught against the chest of an ox of a man whose foul breath, stale with wine and ale, made her feel instantly nauseous.

'What have we here, men? A comely wench—not one of theirs, by the look of her.' A rough hand tore away her cloak, exposing her shapely curves outlined beneath the clinging blue gown. 'And she smells sweet—certainly not one of their stinking brood!'

From within the circle of soldiers, Siward gave an enraged cry and launched himself at the nearest man, who gave a howl of pain and staggered back, blood welling from the gash on his arm. Another, who blocked the Norseman's path to Alisandre and the byre, drove him back.

'Let me go this instant!' Alisandre ordered. Her clenched fists pummelled in vain against her captor's chest. 'My husband will have your head for this. *I* will have your head!'

She flung back her head and stared up into the man's face, and knew great fear at the look she saw in the cruel, narrowed eyes. He wore mail and a halberk, as did the soldiers, but he was clearly the leader—not only from his authoritative tone of voice, but from the richness of his apparel: leather gloves, the backs heavily jewelled, golden buckles fastening the retaining straps of his sword, and the belt which held a jewel-hilted dagger.

'We shall have some sport, after all! We have found a nest of poachers—and we all know what happens to those who poach in the king's forest!' the man proclaimed.

'Are you lacking in brains as well as being blind? Do these men look like poachers?' Alisandre flung back. Everyone was so engrossed in staring at her with rude eyes that made her cheeks blaze with embarrassment, that they were unaware that Cerdic was sidling closer and closer to the byre. Siward had also seen him, but he was in a quandary. If he caused a diversion, he would most certainly be killed, and then both Rollo and Alisandre would be at the mercy of these men. 'These peasants have given us shelter for the night—nothing more. They are under the protection of my husband—Rollo, Duke of Aquitaine. For the harm you do them, or any of us, you will answer to him.'

'And where is your brave husband? Why is he not here to protect his woman?' came the insulting taunt.

When the bearded face loomed closer to hers, Alisandre's fingers groped desperately for the small basilard hidden beneath one of her wide sleeves, and her fingers closed round the hilt. With all her might she pulled it free and plunged it into the man's leg. The restraining arm about her fell away as he staggered back with a howl of pain.

Despite the shock, however, he was swift to retaliate, and a savage blow across the face felled her to the ground. He towered over her, his lips drawn back over yellowed teeth in a leering smile as she tried to scramble to her feet, enjoying the fear rising in her face.

'No woman draws blood on Huw Carradoc!'

'And no man touches the wife of Rollo of Aquitaine, and lives!'

'Rollo!' His name was lost on Alisandre's lips as he launched the throwing-axe from his hand, and the man sank to his knees, the blade buried in his back.

For a moment there was a stunned silence. Then, seeing their leader dead, the soldiers turned, their swords raised. A strange sound like a high-pitched whistle seared the air. The first arrow coming out of the dense trees to the left of the hut dropped the man threatening Cerdic. More arrows came thick and fast and with unerring accuracy. As if in the midst of some horrible nightmare, Alisandre watched men topple and fall and not rise again. A final deadly arrow sped through the air, and the last soldier groaned and reeled off into the bushes, only to collapse before he had reached cover.

'I think Will Appleton has just saved our lives.' And, following Siward's gaze, she saw the man come striding out of the trees, a bow in one hand, an empty quiver slung across his back. 'I was wondering where the rogue had got to!'

'What the devil has been happening here? Where are we?' Rollo demanded harshly. 'I wake to find Berta half dead from fright at my feet, Jarl near suffocating because she has thrust him under my cloak, and my wife about to be violated...' He broke off, his features greying still more, and clutched at Cerdic's arm. 'Get me back inside quickly and bring some food. I'm ravenous!'

Alisandre hurried back into the byre and re-arranged the bed for Rollo to lie on, but he refused to stretch out and ordered himself to be propped up against one of the supporting poles.

'Cerdic, see to Guyon and Gerhard. I think they may be hurt.' She tried to make light of the unpleasant episode, not wanting to think what would have happened if Will Appleton had not arrived on the scene.

He stood just inside the entrance, suspicious-eyed men on each side of him, his thin face impassive as he stared into Rollo's equally doubting face.

Alisandre knew trust would not come easily to either of them. 'My husband and I owe you a debt of gratitude, Will Appleton. We shall not forget what you did for us today. All of us,' she said.

'My men and I are glad to have served you, lady. We enjoy giving Prince John's men a taste of their own.'

'Who are your men?' Rollo demanded. 'Outlaws?'

'Men of no consequence, like myself, lord. But, yes, outlaws, thanks to Prince John's cruelty.'

'Of no consequence to whom?' came back the swift answer. Rollo had seen the deadly accuracy of the longbow, the swiftness with which the arrows came. In his estimation, five or six arrows could be fired at the same time as it took a man to load one bolt into a crossbow. A formidable weapon in the hands of mere peasants!

'Why, to Prince John, of course. Perhaps even to King Richard. We are but Saxons, and he is a Norman more interested in his estates and holdings in France than this land of ours.'

'Prince John obviously thinks a great deal of it, if he is raising men to fight alongside him against King Richard,' Rollo returned, and both Alisandre and Siward looked at him in surprise. He had been delirious when they had talked with Will Appleton, yet he knew. A smile deepened the corners of his mouth. 'Nay, I do not have second sight, but I do remember faces. And a strange tongue. Do you not remember the Welsh mercenaries who fought with Hugo de Greville-Wynter, Siward? The huge bearded one led them, I am sure. So you think you are of no consequence?' He raised his head, and a pair of pale green eyes bored into Will Appleton's weatherbeaten features. 'I could use men like you. I ask no more of you than I am willing to give: your word that if I need men to fight for the true king, you will come when I send for you. In return, I swear to you, no man who has been here today, nor any family, man, woman or child, will suffer at John's hands if it is in my power to prevent it. When King Richard returns, he shall hear of your grievances and deal fairly with every one of you.'

'You know that the king has not yet returned to England?' Alisandre asked.

For a moment, an odd gleam entered his eyes, then he shrugged his shoulders weakly. 'The fever may have sapped my strength, but not my brain! The king should be here, and he is not, so where is he? Mercenaries roam the forests at will and no one attempts to stop them. And Prince John has assumed powers not rightfully belonging to him. Even the simplest man must see that the king's throne is in jeopardy. Sides must be taken. I want to know that I can trust the men at my back!'

The men about Will Appleton exchanged angry glances, for Rollo's meaning was very clear. Another Norman demanding what they were not willing to give!

A look passed between Rollo and Alisandre, and she rose instantly to her feet, knowing he wanted her to take control of the situation. 'You left us, Will Appleton, yet you returned with men to help us. Did you know we would be attacked?'

'Nay, my lady. I brought men to carry your lord to your destination. We have a litter in the trees yonder, although now we shall need more than one. It is not safe here for any of us. We should move quickly.'

'My husband is...' She was about to say 'weak', when she caught Rollo's warning frown, '... in need of nourishment. So is my son.'

'An hour, my lady. It will take us that long to make another litter for your wounded man and to hide the bodies of those carrion outside. We must be well away from here before they are found.'

'Your brother and niece, what will become of them?' Alisandre asked.

'My brother is dead. They cut his throat when we attacked. My niece shall come with me. I can provide for her.'

'No, it is unthinkable that she should live the life of an outlaw. She shall come with me. She shall be my maid, and shall want for nothing ever again,' she promised.

After a moment, he nodded and motioned to his men, and they turned and left.

CHAPTER THREE

ROLLO winced as he moved his head and lay still again. How it throbbed, like a thousand Saracen drums beating in his ears. Had he been wounded? There were no sounds of battle, no singing of birds, restless movements of horses or the normal banter of men after battle. Am I going mad? he wondered. The drums were receding, and in their place—it was not possible!—he could hear a woman softly singing:

'Hush, little baby, now you must sleep.
Mother will watch you, so do not weep.
Sleep—sleep—sleep.'

He knew that voice, that soft, beautiful husky voice that immediately stirred his blood. Karin! No, she was Alisandre now, although to him she would always be his 'little Cat', his Kutti. How many lives had they lost between them? Why did he think of danger? Slowly he stretched, and opened his eyes on to a room darker than he would have expected.

A woman was seated on cushions near a long, narrow window, a child cradled in her arms. Long hair cascaded down over her back to her waist. She wore a gown of grey velvet, the bodice still open, her shoulders bare after feeding the infant. Rollo felt a great ache rise inside him as he watched her, soothed by the gentle voice filled with love, the serene features smiling as they bent to kiss a tiny cheek.

Alarm surged through him, and he struggled to sit up, but could barely raise himself on one elbow, so weak was he. 'Kutti! Help me!'

The cry for help brought her wheeling round. Instantly she was at his side, laying the child at the foot of the bed, then bending over him, restraining hands on his shoulders. Blue eyes clouded with anxiety gazed down into his gaunt, bearded face, and she knelt beside him. 'Lie still, my love. Rest. You are weak.'

'Where are we? I remember little. A hut in the forest—men—graves...' Memory came suddenly flooding back, and he gave a groan. 'Graves! Dear heaven, yes, I remember those. Always graves! Gerhard and the brother of the bowman...'

'Lie still, I beg you. You have been very ill.' Alisandre laid her lips against his heavily bearded cheek, not minding the rough bristles which rubbed against her soft skin.

'How long this time?' Rollo demanded. 'Help me to sit up. I am not dying!'

She smiled at his brusqueness, knowing it was his way of hiding how ill he really felt. He grasped her shoulders as she lifted him—not without difficulty, for he was no lightweight—and arranged the pillows beneath his head. He did not allow her to draw back. His fingers slid over her shoulders, down to her exposed breasts, a scarred thumb teasing the pink nipple still wet with milk, until she gave a soft gasp and allowed him to draw her down against his chest.

'Oh, Rollo, my love, now I know you are mending fast,' she breathed.

He took her mouth, hungry for the taste of her, to touch and know she was real and not a dream. His lips parted hers, his hands stroked and teased, began to push away the material which hid the rest of her body from him—and her senses clamoured for him to release her from the torment she had endured for almost two weeks.

Whereas he had thought for nothing other than possessing her, she was only too aware of Jarl a few feet away, wide awake now and ready to throw a tantrum if she did not settle him at once in the nursery, with Berta to watch over him. It would have been so easy to ignore him, but... 'Rollo—not now, my darling heart—let me see to our son first.'

'Am I to take second place to my son now?' Rollo demanded ungraciously, but he allowed her to draw back and rearrange her clothing.

'He is the most important thing in your life,' she replied quietly, and a gleam sprang to the green eyes watching her. She had to jump back to avoid the hand which tried to grasp her again.

'Come here, and I will prove otherwise. Coward!' he chided, as she opened the door and called for Berta.

'Tonight you will pay for those words, my husband,' she flung back at him, knowing that she was well out of reach and he too weak to get out of bed and come after her. 'If you are strong enough!'

'I can still clip your claws, Kutti. And you will enjoy it.'

'I shall indeed.' Once she would not have engaged in such banter with him and her cheeks would have fired with embarrassed colour, but not now—they had shared too much.

At times like these he could not imagine things being different between them, never doubting her love, never regretting the road he had taken. Perhaps he had been right to bring her here. In time, he would be able to tell her the real reason and ask her forgiveness for his deception. When it was safe—and they were back where they belonged.

'Show me my son,' he said, and she lifted Jarl and laid him in his arms. 'Am I imagining it, or has he grown? How long have I been here? This—is Wynterfold?'

'Yes. For a week. You—You collapsed as Will and the others laid you in the litter. It is small wonder—you had so little strength. Yet you saved me my love, and more than just my life, with the throwing of your axe. God was with us that day. You developed chills and a fever the day after we arrived, and you have been delirious at times ever since. I would not allow the doctor to bleed you,' she added.

'Thank God for that! I have lost enough of my blood to the Saracens to need all I have left.' Jarl lifted a chubby finger and touched the growth of beard on Rollo's chin and immediately withdrew it, his face puckering into an expression of distaste. 'Is he going to cry?' Rollo's love for his son was undisputed, but he still felt awkward at times, holding the child. He was so tiny, so delicate, so precious—and *he* was so clumsy. He was more accustomed to having a sword or an axe in his hand than a baby.

'He does not like your beard,' Alisandre laughed softly. How she enjoyed seeing them together, watching the pride grow on her husband's face as he studied his son, the love which he could not hide in the depths of his eyes. Moments like this always brought them closer together.

'No more do I. It feels like a hawthorn bush— prickly, like me.'

'Nay, more like an oak, with a little willow thrown in.'

'Have I begun to bend, Kutti? Or am I still the ogre who found you in Acre? Made you mine against your will?'

'Against my will? Am I not here with you now? I have no chains binding me, except those of love. Love is the key, my husband, to your heart and to mine. To those who love as we do, nothing is denied. All we have to do is reach out and take what is ours.'

'And in doing so, might we not offend others?' It worried him when she spoke thus. She was so con- fident—of herself and of him!

'We have the three of us. We come before all others,' she told him without hesitation.

'Before king? And country? Before loyalty?' he challenged.

'Yes, before all of these.' Again she did not hesitate, although she knew all three were of great importance to him. 'While we are together and our love binds us, nothing can part us, or destroy us.'

'If only life were as simple as that, Kutti!' Then he asked, with a frown, 'How was our reception here?'

'Not at all as I expected,' Alisandre confessed. 'Cousin Margaret has been more than kind and helpful—so understanding.'

'This is your house—your estate—your inheritance,' he reminded her. 'How could she be anything else?'

'I find her greatly changed—or perhaps it is because I have grown up. As a child, I used to walk in her shadow. Whenever she came to visit Wynterfold, I used to run and hide until I found what kind of mood she was in. She could be very—cruel. Yes, that is the right word. Always she was so confident, far older in her years than she should have been, and she—she liked the young men too much. They would flock round her like sheep, flattered by a look, a kind word or a kiss. She was very free with those. My uncle once whipped a stable-boy to death because he found them together in one of the barns. She swore the boy had dragged her in there and tried to make her submit to him ... Everyone believed her.'

'Except you.'

'Perhaps she did not realise how attractive she was then—men seemed drawn to her. She is even more beautiful now, but gentle in her ways—and so considerate. She is packing to leave, although she has nowhere of her own to go, because I have returned. She said Wynterfold was mine, and yours—to share; that she would feel an intruder if she remained.'

'What of her father's house and lands?'

'Apparently Hugo sold them to raise money to buy men for King Richard's cause.'

'He spent damned little of it on men or armour, or food! His men had to provide for themselves, most of the time.' Rollo did not like what he had heard.

'I—I should like to tell her she can stay—for a while, at least,' Alisandre said hesitantly. 'She can have rooms on the far side of the house, away from us, and her own servants. I shall engage others if they are not suitable. The house is large enough for us all, my love. I am sure it would not be for long.'

'Another woman would be company for you while I am away.' He nodded, and saw the smile fade from her face as she realised he was referring to the time when he would return to France, to Verduse. Quickly he added, 'That will not be for some considerable time if I am not to be fed properly!' Then a smile lit her face, and he looked at her questioningly.

'I was wondering, now you are better, whether I should dine below with my cousin tonight. We have hardly had a chance to talk since I arrived.'

'I shall spare you for an hour or two—no longer— if you really need to chatter,' Rollo said grudgingly. His fingers caught her chin, turning her face this way and that, lightly gliding down over her throat.

'The bruises have gone. You lied to me, did you not? I tried to kill you. I remember that, if little else. I thought you were . . . Lisette.'

The name did not come easily to his lips, and her hand covered his, not wanting him to dwell on the moment. 'You were not yourself. Besides, Siward was near. I know you could never harm me—not intentionally.'

'Then you still do not know me! I have the devil's own temper, and my moods come straight from Hades itself. You have seen them, heard me when I am in the midst of that darkness. Such a thin line separates love and hate...'

'Do not torture yourself one instant longer. Sleep. Tonight I shall show you nothing has changed between us, my husband.'

'When I wake, bring this Will Appleton to me. I wish to thank him for what he did that day.' Instantly he saw Alisandre's face cloud. 'What is it? You are keeping something from me. Out with it, Kutti.'

'Will Appleton and his men came no further than in sight of the house. Siward fetched servants to carry you the rest of the way. They just—disappeared. One moment they were all around us, the next, gone! Vanished back into the trees like—like shadows. All of them are outlaws—"a wolf's head" was how Will described himself, because anyone can legally kill him. It's monstrous.'

'Is there more?' Instinctively Rollo knew she was holding something back.

'King Richard...' He sat bolt upright in bed, the colour draining from his cheeks. 'He has been imprisoned by Leopold of Austria. We heard two days ago, but it would seem that Prince John has known far longer. He is in London at this very moment trying to raise an army to steal the king's throne. He has issued a proclamation stating that his brother died in prison from a fever he caught in the Holy Land. No one knows what to believe. The king was very ill before he left. Perhaps . . .'

'No!' Rollo thundered.

'I agree, but there are so many confusing reports from all over the country of people who say they have seen the king. Others say he was drowned when his ship was blown ashore for the second time. He had taken passage aboard a corsair ship at Corfu, to travel overland afterwards, I suppose.'

'I must know. I must.' The ferocity of Rollo's tone alarmed her. 'Siward must go to London at once and find out the truth. If he is a prisoner, there will be a ransom demand. Leopold of Austria has no love for the king of England, but he will not kill him. He will ask a high price for his release. He has not forgotten Acre. Send Siward to me—now—Kutti.' It was a command, not a request, and she knew better than to disobey. He would not rest until he knew the truth.

'Am I interrupting?' Lady Margaret stood just inside the doorway. Neither had heard her knock or seen her enter. 'I came to see how the patient was. Your maid told me he is fast recovering his faculties, Alisandre. I am so pleased.'

She was tall for a woman, Rollo saw, as she advanced towards the bed, not waiting for an invitation. And strikingly beautiful—Alisandre had been right, there—but not in the way that his wife was. Her shining black hair was plaited and coiled on the crown of her head, barely covered by a snowy white wimple perched on the top of a jewelled circlet. But there was a hardness in the eyes which did not go with the smile bestowed upon him, or with the full sensuous mouth, deepening as he held her bold gaze with eyes that were as searching as her own. A strange colour—large violet pools, fringed with sooty lashes. Her skin was flawless, like alabaster. He preferred Alisandre's softly tanned complexion. The gown of bright red wool she wore, with an overdress of the same colour, woven with gold thread, did justice to the full breasts and hips. He saw nothing to make him take an instant dislike to her—but he did. Every nerve in his body shrank from her as if she was some apparition of evil. He sensed great danger, without knowing why.

'Rollo!' Alisandre was staring at him, puzzled by his bad manners. 'This is my cousin Margaret. I think you have mesmerised him, cousin. He has lost his tongue!'

'I have heard that the Lord of Darkness can be mesmerised by only one woman,' Margaret said with a laugh—and it was as if a spell was suddenly broken, releasing Rollo to find his voice again. 'Welcome to Wynterfold, my lord.'

He was imagining things! The eyes were gentle now, and concerned, as they looked down at him, the cultured voice was warm and friendly; yet, for a moment...

'In truth, you are correct.' He was himself again. 'There is not a woman in this world who could turn my head after Alisandre.'

'I am told harem women are taught many tricks with which to hold a man. One day you must enlighten me, cousin. Oh, dear, forgive me! My thoughtless tongue. I did not mean that to sound as it did . . .'

At her words, Alisandre had sucked in her breath and stiffened visibly. An expletive broke from beneath her husband's breath, and his fists clenched. Quickly she sought to pass over the mistake, for she was sure it was nothing more. It was only natural for Margaret to be curious about her missing years.

'One day, perhaps.' She forced a smile to stiff lips.

'My dear, I have offended you. My tongue will be the death of me, but I am so glad to have another woman to talk to that I became carried away. Please, say you forgive me? Dine downstairs with us later and let me make up for my stupidity. Since Hugo left, I rarely see anyone who can indulge in small talk, and heaven only knows I would be grateful for that, let alone an intelligent conversation!'

'I understand,' Alisandre replied, remembering how she and Berengaria had spent hours closeted together. 'It must be lonely for you.'

'You are aware that I was responsible for your brother's death,' Rollo said harshly, unexpectedly, stunning Alisandre.

'The news was brought to me by Roger Chabret, one of his companions in the Holy Land. He is here at Wynterfold now, and rides to London to Prince John's court. Yes, my lord, I am fully aware of it, and I bear you no ill feeling. My brother could be a cruel man—and there were times when I despised him. I loved him, too, that never changed, but he . . .' She shrugged her shoulders, a sad smile stealing across her lovely face. 'I know, too, that he would have asked for Alisandre's life in order to keep Wynterfold. That was the extent of his ambition. He could never give up anything that had once belonged to him. I do not have that failing, I am glad to say. I shall leave at the end of the week. Wynterfold will once more belong to you, cousin Alisandre.'

'It always did,' Rollo reminded her. He was not imagining things now. Those eyes contained the venom of a snake as they momentarily swept over him. He would be relieved to see the back of her. Before he could utter another word, Alisandre broke in.

'No, cousin, stay. As long as it pleases you. Consider this your home until you find somewhere else. It would be uncharitable of us to insist you leave. Stay, and allow me to repay you for caring so diligently for my home during my absence. I insist,' she added, as Margaret seemed to waver.

'Only if your husband also insists. To stay, and not to be welcome...'

'Accept my wife's generosity while you can, Lady Margaret. No doubt she will find it—useful—to have another woman about the place. She has been away a long time, and will need your counsel on matters relating to the estate until she feels capable of taking charge herself. You will find her quick to learn.'

As I am, he thought, as Alisandre escorted the woman to the door, assuring her that she would be pleased to dine with her and their guest, Roger Chabret. I was not wrong! You are evil.

'Find me Siward, Kutti,' he ordered, not giving her a chance to chide him for his ungracious manner. Let her believe it was because he was still tired and weak and not accustomed to entertaining from a sick-bed. Anything, so that he did not have to tell her now that the lady was not all she appeared to be. He would stake his life on it. When he remembered Huw Carradoc, he wondered if that was not exactly what he was doing. And not only his! 'And bring me writing materials.'

'Rollo?' One look, and she hurried from the room without further protest.

The Great Hall was ablaze with light from a hundred or more candles and wall torches, a fire burned in the chasm of a fireplace set in a huge recess in one of the six-foot-thick walls, and heavy shutters bolted against all the windows shut out a windswept night, bleak and cold, with frost already in the air.

Many of the windows now had glass in them as well as the stout shutters. The bedrooms had feather mattresses, and curtains about the beds for privacy. There were tapestries on the walls of most rooms, and sweet-smelling rushes and bowls of herbs from the garden to soften the smell of damp that rose each year from the depths of the keep. Most of the rooms now had their own garderobes and stone washbasins or a pitcher and bowl. Her cousin, or both her cousins, Margaret and Hugo, had spent a great deal on enlarging and improving the house over the past years.

'Everything is to your satisfaction, cousin?' Margaret inclined her head in Alisandre's direction, one dark eyebrow arched as she refused a portion of plums marinaded in wine. 'If the food is not to your liking, you have only to tell the cook your own requirements. Under the circumstances—with you spending so much time with your husband—I naturally undertook to continue running the house and all it entails. I know, of course, that you are anxious to assume full control, as is your right . . .'

'Cousin Margaret, stop! I cannot eat another mouthful; that is the only reason for my refusal. You have a marvellous cook, and all your servants are without fault,' Alisandre protested, not wanting her cousin to think her ungrateful for all that had been, and was being, done for her.

'*Your* cook, cousin. *Your* servants, now. I have merely been, shall we say, standing in for you here as mistress.'

'And well you have done! I fear I shall never attain your skills. You are always so capable, and so good with people. I shall be a mere shadow in your wake.'

'But you have never had to deal with a household like this! Lazy devils, most of them. Thieves! They will rob you blind if you do not watch them every moment of the day. In the Holy Land they would have had their feet ripped raw by the bastinado, or their hands cut off, would they not, Lady Alisandre? Now that is something I am certain you *do* understand after your years with the Infidels. Complete obedience to one master or mistress—or punishment of the cruellest kind, even death.'

Alisandre felt, rather than saw, Siward stiffen at the insolent words from Roger Chabret seated on her left. She did not remember him as being part of her cousin Hugo's entourage of knights, for she had not been directly involved with any of them. Rollo had seen to that.

He looked three or four years younger than Margaret, despite a slight greying of the long brown hair curling about his shoulders and flecks of it in his beard. He had grown that to try to hide the ugly scar which seared one cheek from ear to mouth, she decided. His yellow eyes, considering her as she neared the dais, had made her steps falter—she, who was so proud and in command of her own life—and instantly Siward had been beside her, his arm outstretched. Gratefully she had accepted the additional support and taken her place at the table.

'Roger, you must not talk of those times. It upsets my cousin deeply. Understandably so. The poor child has been through hell,' Margaret chided him.

'On the contrary, I was cared for by a good man who loved me as his own daughter. I was treated as a princess, with my own household.' The words were out before she could contain them. She was not ashamed of those years, so why should she deny them? 'I was taught by one of Saladin's own astrologers.'

'How fortunate to have fallen into the—right hands,' Margaret answered, her violet eyes widening as she considered Alisandre's words. 'When Roger brought the news that you were still alive, I could scarcely believe it. We have heard such terrible tales of the things they do to women captives.'

'As you say, I was indeed fortunate.'

'And you actually met—that—that creature Saladin?' her cousin added. What a child Alisandre still was, for all her tuition! To speak openly of her years with the very people who had taken the lives of countless brave Englishmen, not to mention the other nationalities who had flocked to join the Third Crusade in all its holy glory. To declare the Infidel a friend . . . Why, she should be torn to pieces! At the very least, shunned by everyone of importance, rejected by the women, scorned as a common trollop by the men. In a few months, if Margaret had her way, Alisandre would regret having returned to Wynterfold.

'He was a great man, one of the wisest I have ever known. And I must confess there have been very few.' She ignored the leer which crept across Roger Chabret's face. 'If only he and King Richard had met face to face and discussed their problems, I am sure they could have been resolved without more bloodshed.'

Margaret gave a shrug of her shoulders and rose. 'Tomorrow we shall be leaving for London. I have business there which may take a week, perhaps more. I am sure you will not be averse to being alone with your husband for a little while, and it will also give you an opportunity to reacquaint yourself with the everyday running of Wynterfold. My bailiff will be on hand, first thing in the morning, to tell you anything you need to know. I shall not be leaving until mid-morning, so we shall see each other before I go.'

'Perhaps I might ride with you, Lady Margaret?' Alisandre looked up at Siward, agape at his request. Why should he want to go to London? Rollo was not strong enough to leave his bed, and his lord's protection was his personal responsibility. 'I have an errand for my Lord Rollo and would be glad of the company, especially as I am a stranger in your country.'

'I shall be glad of some civilised conversation— Siward, is it?'

'Ay, my lady. My family were Norsemen who settled in Normandy.'

'How interesting. Your ancestors have plundered these shores for years. Now, of course, we have Normans.' For a brief moment she stared down at Roger Chabret, whose head had fallen on to the table, then slowly considered the tall, hard-faced man. A challenge, she decided. She liked what she saw, despite his obvious peasant background, and what did that matter? She was tired of boys like Roger, who fawned over her and expected her to be faithful to them, and rich courtiers who showered her with gifts and proposed marriage. Marriage! She would never be owned by any man, or bound by meaningless vows. She had the protection of the most important man in the land, and even he knew he could not hold her. Both being of a totally selfish nature, the casual relationship was more than satisfying, and for her, profitable.

Yes, the Norseman would be an interesting challenge, but his interest lay elsewhere. She had known that the moment she saw Alisandre lay her hand on his arm. The tightening of his cheek muscles—a look of pain in his eyes. He could not stand her touching him! And not because he disliked her, oh no! Margaret had seen the way his eyes followed her. She knew she now possessed the knowledge that could be instrumental in destroying first Alisandre, for daring to come back and assume that she was still mistress of Wynterfold, and then the creature with her, who called himself the Lord of Darkness. She would send him into the darkest void he had ever known for killing her beloved brother!

'Why are you going to London, Siward? I—we—need you here,' Alisandre asked, as they climbed the stairs to the upper floor which contained the bedrooms.

'As I have explained, my lady, I have something to do for Lord Rollo.' She knew that stubborn expression on his face. It told her she would learn nothing more from him.

'Very well. I will ask my husband.' She was slightly annoyed that he would not confide in her.

'Better you should do so when you are alone.'

'Alone? Have we important secrets here that no one else must hear?' she chided.

'Important to some, perhaps.' He opened the door to Rollo's room and, as she entered, a pace behind, he said quietly. 'It is Siward, my lord, and the Lady Alisandre.'

Candles set each side of the bed illuminated the man sitting upright in the bed, a dagger poised to hurl at the shadowy doorway, and the dark, set features behind the gleaming blade. It was clear why Siward had thought it necessary to announce their entrance. He had known what was awaiting them. Both men were acting as if some terrible danger lurked in every corner. Who was there at Wynterfold to harm any of them?

'I am unarmed,' she said, lifting one of her wide sleeves so that he could see she did not carry the basilard with her tonight, and her husband's lips deepened into a smile at the light mockery in her tone. 'Had I known we were in danger...'

'You have dined well?' The dagger disappeared beneath his pillows and he settled back again, her pointed words ignored.

'Cousin Margaret is a gracious hostess, and we have eaten like royalty, have we not, Siward?'

'Indeed we have. I leave mid-morning with the Lady Margaret,' he said, preparing to take his leave.

Alisandre had seated herself on a stool before a brass-bound wall mirror, and was beginning to unbraid her hair. He watched as the red gold tresses, freed from the confines of the ribbons which had bound them in place, tumbled about her shoulders in a profusion of waves. She was still as inaccessible to him as she had always been, and always would be. The journey to London was a blessing—even if it was in the company of an odious, loud-mouthed man and a woman whose eyes were too bold for his liking. The offered diversion might just give him time to regain control of himself, to return and be able to tell her— to tell Rollo—of his desire to leave his service. 'If you require nothing further, my lord, I will look in on the men before I retire.'

'We have all we need.' Rollo's eyes were on his wife as he spoke, watching her deftly using a silver-backed brush on her hair. Her eyes met and held his, and the smile which came to her lips was for him alone. Neither even noticed Siward closing the door.

'Why is Siward to go to London?'

'Are you so loath to be alone with me, Kutti?' Rollo asked quietly.

'Alone? With Gy and Guyon, not to mention your very demanding son, Jarl?' Alisandre laughed.

'We are alone now, but I am in a warm bed and you are shivering over there. Come to bed and let me warm you. And I shall answer all your inquisitive questions.'

Alisandre felt his eyes boring into her back as she rose and began to unfasten her surcoat. As she slipped it over her head and turned towards him, she saw the hunger in them and caught her breath at the intensity of his desire. Excitement stirred inside her and her fingers trembled as she loosened the fastenings at the side of her gown, pushed it away and stepped out of it. The last of her undergarments fell in a huddle about her feet.

'Let me look at you a moment,' Rollo said hoarsely. The birth of Jarl had not thickened her figure; in fact her breasts and thighs had become firmer, he thought, her stomach once again taut. Her legs were long and slender, her waist almost back to its previous size. He threw aside the bedcovers and she came to him gladly, snuggling against his chest as he brought them back over them both and then entwined his arms about her. To look at her had aroused his manhood, to hold her brought him to the heights of impatience, but Alisandre was not about to let him forget that he had questions to answer.

'About Siward—you promised...' she murmured, as his lips travelled down over her throat to her shoulder and breast. 'What is this secrecy between you?'

'A precaution, my love, nothing more. I must know if Richard is alive or dead. If dead, then John must never take the throne, for it rightfully belongs to Richard's successor, Arthur of Brittany. And if he still lives, money must be raised to get him out of prison. I have to hear the news, whatever it is, from someone I can trust.'

'And so you send Siward. That I understand, but to whom? We know no one at court who can be of help.'

'A few of my friends in the Holy Land have returned home. Besides, I have...a name. Such men are loyal to their rightful king. Kutti, these things are not for women. Have you not enough to occupy your mind here at Wynterfold? With your cousin gone, you must assume control again as mistress of this house. You will be kept busy—too busy to bother your head about other matters.'

'The return of the king is my concern, too,' she insisted. 'Your troubles are mine.' Was she right in the belief that he had known of Margaret's departure before she had?

'Then remember the first duty of a wife,' he teased, his hands cupping her breasts, exploring the fullness of them, the softness, lowering his head to kiss each one in turn. 'I am dying for want of you.'

'I am pleased to hear it.' Gy or Siward, had brought him information, she suspected. Why had he not asked her?

'Satisfy this hunger if you can, witch!' he challenged her and the blue eyes which looked at him now were filled with love. Lifting her arms she clasped them behind his neck, allowing him to roll her on to her back and move his body over hers to enter her. So strong, despite the illness that had plagued him, and which would have completely sapped the strength from a lesser man, she thought, as he began to move inside her, and she was consumed by fire.

CHAPTER FOUR

'I INTEND to ride to the village this afternoon and make myself known there again,' Alisandre said, swathing herself in a heavy cloak. The weather was not improving and snow had begun to fall early that morning. 'I could leave it for a few more days, if you think you should come with me.'

'Wynterfold is your concern, Kutti. I am well content to leave the running of it in your capable hands. From all I hear, your return is welcomed in all quarters. Cousin Margaret has a temper that has earned her many enemies, and her relationship with the king's brother has kept her coffers well filled when less fortunate people have lost everything. A woman with foresight.'

'You are most unfair to her!' Alisandre protested indignantly. 'She is a woman alone who must protect herself as best she can, and what better way to do it than to have friends in high places? Are men not equally concerned about such things? Siward does not like her, I know.'

'Nor has he spoken of her to me; it was Gy who told me the gossip. He has found himself a sewing-maid who is fascinated by his big brown eyes, have you not, you young rogue?' Rollo said with a chuckle, and the squire's cheeks grew red with embarrassment as Alisandre's eyes fixed on him accusingly.

'She's a plague on my life, my lord. She won't leave me alone.'

'But a veritable source of information which could be useful to me. You will have to suffer a while longer, lad.'

'Yes, my lord,' Gy muttered, but it was obvious by his tone that the prospect of further 'suffering' did not unduly worry him.

'Why all this secrecy, this desire for information?' she demanded, as she and Rollo went downstairs to say goodbye to Margaret. 'First Siward, and now you. If you need information, surely you have only to ask the servants? You are treating them like—like enemies.'

'That is exactly how I consider them until I know where their allegiance lies—with King Richard or his brother John. Have you forgotten how close your cousin is rumoured to be to John? Her word carries no weight at Wynterfold now that you have returned. If money is raised, or men, it will be for the rightful king of this land. Do you not think that places you—all of us, indeed—in danger? I do. My instincts tell me that that woman would turn on you if she thought you stood in the way of what she wants.'

'I don't understand your dislike of her. Or perhaps I do...' Alisandre broke off as he looked down at her, and the anger in the depths of his pale green eyes stilled further comment. She had been about to mention his first wife, and he knew it.

'It has nothing to do with the past, Kutti, believe me.'

'Can you deny that your thoughts have been occupied with the past ever since we were in France, at Verduse? She was in your mind when you were ill, dominating your thoughts, even at a time like that. If you believe we are in danger, why did we ever come here? Margaret can have Wynterfold, for all I care...' Again she broke off, unwilling to continue, and anger him further. Now that they had a chance to be alone for the first time since arriving in England, she did not want that to happen.

By the door of the Great Hall, Rollo paused, and drew her back into one of the many deep recesses that lined the walls. 'I want only to be with you, to enjoy these days before your cousin returns and Siward brings me news I do not want to hear. Did you not tell me that we come before all others? Let it be like that for as long as possible. No tomorrows for us, only today!'

Was that not what she, too, wanted? Oblivious of servants coming and going through the door with luggage and last-minute items for the journey, she lifted her face to his. He kissed her with unexpected passion, holding her so tightly against his chest that she could hardly breathe. She had felt the same urgency in him the night before when they had made love, and early this morning he had awoken her with his insistent caresses and laughed at her drowsy protests and taken her while she was still half asleep, as if every moment was of great importance, not to be wasted.

She laid a hand on his arm, and they went out into the grey morning.

Her cousin was huddled into a heavy cloak of deep violet velvet, inspecting the baggage-cart laden outside the main storerooms. The fur lining the cowl and bordering the edge had been dyed to match. She looked exquisite, Alisandre thought, suddenly aware, because she had overslept, of how her own hair was loose beneath the hood of her cloak and she had snatched the first dress in the closet.

'Cousin Margaret, are you sure you want to leave in this weather? I am sure it will snow quite heavily before nightfall.'

'If that happens, I shall find the most comfortable lodgings I can, and wait for better weather.' Margaret bestowed a dazzling smile on her. 'The house is yours, cousin. My one request is that I do not return to find I have been allocated new rooms. I have spent the past year ensuring that mine are the most comfortable in the house. If I am to stay, I would like to remain where I am.'

'I would not dream of having you moved,' Alisandre protested. 'Whatever can you think of me to suggest such a thing?'

'You are mistress here now, so it is only natural for you to want the best accommodation.'

'Nothing will be changed, I assure you,' Alisandre began, and then became aware of a frown puckering Rollo's brows. 'I shall, of course, make other alterations elsewhere in the house to accommodate my husband and myself more suitably, as we are a family, but I am sure you will find them to your liking.'

Assert yourself! Be more positive! That was what her husband's frown indicated, and she tried hard to equal his expectations. But it was difficult with Margaret, who had done so much and asked so little.

Twenty men at arms were checking girths and saddles outside the stables, but not until Margaret's horse was brought and a groom had helped her to mount did they also mount and group in an orderly formation behind her. And only then did Roger Chabret appear from the house, in mail and halberk, as if he were prepared for battle, Alisandre thought, her features tightening at the sight of him.

'Lady Alisandre.' The gallant bow he performed before her, the careful way he took her hand and touched her fingers to his lips, took her completely by surprise. 'Before I leave, I must thank you for your hospitality. I am your humble servant, Lady Alisandre.'

'Damn the man's insolence!' Rollo said harshly as the cavalcade moved out of sight, Siward leaving last of all.

'Must you believe the worst of everyone?' Alisandre asked in annoyance. She had assumed his impatience to be due to inactivity and a long—at least for him—confinement to bed. Now she was wondering if he was not over-anxious to return to Verduse. It was plain that he did not like England, or

Wynterfold, or Margaret, or Roger Chabret. He was in an impossible mood!

'You have much to learn, Kutti. You are still young, and inexperienced in the devious natures of men— and women—in treachery.'

'I learned a great deal about deviousness and treachery in Acre, my lord!' The words were uttered before she could contain them, and once said, they could not be retracted. His pale eyes glittered as they considered her, challenged her to attribute either of those descriptions to him or to what had passed between them in that city. Without a word, he turned and walked away, and words of abject apology died on her lips. She had not meant it as a slight against him.

She stood in the cold, waiting until she had sufficiently recovered her composure to go into the Great Hall, where the steward of Wynterfold and all the servants were gathered, according to her wishes. She wanted to see them all and get to know them personally, so that they would come to accept her as mistress. For over an hour she spoke with them, and then asked the steward, a man named Ponsford, to show her over the house and the outbuildings so that she could see for herself the extent of Wynterfold's potentiality.

'Where is my husband?' she asked Gy, when she entered the house at the end of her inspection.

'Practising with the Guard, my lady. He has instructed a quintain to be built, but until it is ready, he intends everyone to make the most of their idle time: an hour every morning and afternoon with all weapons.'

'He has eaten?' It was well past the time for the main meal. What should she do? Alisandre wondered. Interrupt him and further aggravate his mood, or leave him . . . ?

'Nay, he has no need of food. The sword and axe he wields are food enough for him,' Gy returned with a grin. 'His strength has returned, my lady. You should have seen the way he knocked Cerdic to the ground . . . and Guyon could not last a minute with him!'

'Would that Siward were here to match him,' Alisandre murmured, 'and make him realise he is not yet strong enough to exert himself thus. I shall ride to the village to see conditions there for myself, but be back before dark.'

The steward was waiting for her. Ponsford was a portly, short man who had to be assisted into the saddle by one of the grooms, who was almost crushed in the process. She liked him. He answered all her questions without hesitation. He had served Margaret, but he was also willing to serve his new mistress without reserve, and that pleased her. He was good at his job. She needed someone like this to help her in the months to come. If there was a slight hesitation in his answers when the subject turned to her cousin, she dismissed this as a natural reluctance to speak ill of the mistress he had served long before she brought him to Wynterfold, to assume control of her household.

The village was not at all as she expected. A huddle of houses, mainly of wattle and daub, supported by timber frames. Fewer than she remembered as a girl, when she had ridden through it with her parents. Scrawny chickens pecked at the frozen earth; the poverty was obvious of the men and women who came out of their homes to gaze at her curiously and then turn and talk among themselves. She turned expectantly to Ponsford, and the man lifted his shoulders and shook his head. Her mouth tightened.

'That tells me nothing. These people are starving. Why?'

'They are too lazy to grow crops for themselves, my lady. They rely on the goodwill of the Lady Margaret, begging at her door when the fancy takes them.'

'Liar!' A long-haired bearded man in his early twenties came close to her horse and caught the bridle so that she could not turn away. 'We are starving because the great lady of Wynterfold prefers to be in the bed of Prince John rather than attending to matters here! Our oxen were taken to raise money for that brother of hers for the Crusade, God damn him to hell! He took all the able-bodied men from the village, and only three have returned. This village is a village of widows and orphans. What are you going to do about that—you and your Norman lord?' He spat on the ground with vicious contempt.

Ponsford kneed his mount between them, forcing the man to relinquish his hold on her bridle, deliberately forcing him off balance so that he fell to the ground.

'Enough!' Had she not called out, she suspected he might have trampled the unfortunate fellow, so bleak were his features.

'He does not know to whom he speaks, my lady! He must be taught manners.'

'First let us show him *our* manners, that he may learn,' she said firmly, and reluctantly he backed his horse away.

'What is your name?' she asked the man, who glowered at her even though he was flat on his back and vulnerable.

'Thomas Luckett. My mother brought you into the world, my lady. She suckled you when your own mother had no milk.'

'Elfleda's son! Have you no work at the house with your mother? Your father was the finest saddler in this part of the country. Where is he now?' How strange she could remember that!

'Dead—he fell at the walls of Acre. Where were you, lady, when he died with a Saracen arrow in his chest? Tending the fine warrior who aimed it, perhaps?'

Alisandre blenched. They knew! She could see the accusation in every face. She gathered the reins tightly in one hand, about to turn her horse and escape from those hostile faces, and then paused. Into her mind came the wise words of Tamir Ibn Dak, her old teacher. 'When an arrow takes flight, it will find its mark. If a fool takes flight, he may run for ever...and ever.' If she turned away now from this challenge, took flight, where would it end? She had to make a stand from the very beginning. How dared these peasants stand in judgement of her? They knew nothing. She looked down into Thomas's face, her own a tight mask of pain.

'Perhaps I was. At that time, I had no memory, no recollection of who or what I was. Had it not been for my husband, Rollo, Duke of Aquitaine, I might still be in Acre in a stinking cell, or dead, my head forfeit because my very own cousin Hugo de Greville-Wynter needed that in order to retain control of these estates—my estates, my inheritance! Mine, do you hear me, every one of you? These belong to me, and by God, they will always belong to me. They were my father's before me, they will belong to my son, and they will be well guarded, believe me. If you do not like what you see before you, you may get yourselves gone from my sight, *and* from Wynterfold. If you stay, I want to hear no more of this talk. The war is over. We are at peace in the Holy Land, and soon King Richard will return.'

'How can he, when he lies in an Austrian dungeon?' a man called from the back of the crowd.

'That matter is in hand. There will be a ransom, and the people of England will raise it to bring him home.'

'Richard's home?' Luckett scoffed. 'He cares nothing for this land.'

'Do you prefer Prince John, with his taxes and his quest for the throne? Do you want to see this land in

turmoil for years to come? It will be, if you do not
rally to the king,' Alisandre snapped, angered by their
apathy. 'Look at you! Half starved and complaining,
and yet not willing to lift a finger to do anything for
yourselves.'

'If we could, the Lady Margaret would not let us.
We were useful only when she wanted the fields
ploughed and seeds sown. She does not want men who
can think for themselves. That's why the whole of
Wynterfold was emptied of your father's servants and
retainers when she came here. She wants those about
her who will fawn and bow whenever she passes—and
share her bed when the prince is not about...'

'You go too far!' Ponsford grated.

'Yes, he does,' Alisandre agreed. 'So he shall have
the chance to prove the worth of his words. You will
come to Wynterfold tomorrow, in the morning, and
you will tell me of your grievances. And I shall require proof. I am no addle-brained child to be taken
in simply by what you have said. Proof, do you hear
me! And your mother will be present while you speak.
If I remember correctly, she can wield a brush with
such devastation that no one is safe when her temper
is aroused! If you lie to me...'

'And once inside Wynterfold, where shall I end up?
I hear the dungeons are very deep and damp. A man
can languish there for years without proper
nourishment or care. Why should I trust you?'

'Find a reason. The truth, perhaps?'

As she wheeled her horse about, she fixed Ponsford
with a piercing look, her blue eyes as cold as the

snowflakes beginning to settle about her shoulders. 'Open the storerooms at Wynterfold and bring these people food. Meat, and flour to bake fresh bread. Whatever is necessary, do you understand?'

'But—But...' Ponsford stuttered, thinking of Lady Margaret's likely reaction to such an act. 'We shall need all the food we have for winter.'

'If you do not do exactly as I order and bring the food to these people by morning, I shall find myself another steward,' Alisandre said. 'The matter is closed.'

'You did not tell me you had trouble in the village the other day,' Rollo said one morning, as he watched the maid braid his wife's hair.

'Did I not?' Alisandre looked at him through the mirror, wondering why he had lingered so long with her this morning. They had spent less time together since her cousin's departure, instead of more. She would have dearly loved to have lain in his arms at night and told him how successfully she was running the house. The villagers would depend on her, in time, as they should have done with Margaret. The things she had heard had silently shocked her, yet she had managed to convey no emotion, display no feelings of anger or distaste as her old nurse, Elfleda, and her son, Thomas Luckett, told her of the years since Hugo and his sister had assumed control of Wynterfold. Both had been hated, feared and cursed daily by those in their employ for their cruelty and immoral way of life. Alisandre knew she would have to tax her cousin on what she had learned for her own peace of mind.

'Well?' Rollo demanded, climbing to his feet.

'Had there been trouble, my love, I would have told you. Let us call it a misunderstanding.'

'To be threatened by one of your own peasants?' In trying to make her more self-confident and self-sufficient for when he was absent, Rollo realised he was placing a barrier between them. Gradually she would need his advice less and less.

'That has all been resolved. The villagers have just cause for their grievances, and I shall take up the matter with cousin Margaret when she returns from London,' Alisandre returned with a smile.

'What are you doing this morning? I thought we might go hawking together. I have acquired a new falcon.'

'I am sorry, Rollo, but Ponsford and I have arranged to go over the ledgers for the estate. From what he tells me, there has been a great deal of over-spending on trivialities, and that must be rectified. If he is right in his assumptions, we are living on the charity of Prince John.'

'I have more than enough money for your needs,' Rollo said, his tone sharper than he intended.

'Thank you. I shall remember that, should the need arise.' She had acquired a new stature from her position, he thought, as she rose and the maid swathed her in a warm cloak. Would she come to consider possessions and money—a name, his name—more important to her than what they had shared?

* * *

'You look tired, my love.' Alisandre rose to her feet, putting aside her embroidery as Rollo entered the room and cast down his cloak and gloves into a nearby chair. It was dark outside. The Great Hall, on her instructions, had not been laid for them tonight, and he made it clear that he had noticed.

'I am hungry, Kutti. What are you up to? No food awaits me, and you are occupying yourself up here.'

'When I should be awaiting my lord and master?' Her tone was all sweetness, honeyed by the thought of what she had prepared. She ignored his frown. 'That is what I am doing. Come, a hot bath is ready for you. Soak away the strains of the day, and then we will eat.'

Without giving him a chance to argue, she pulled aside the curtain separating their bedroom from the antechamber beyond, and went inside. He followed, and saw the iron tub which had been prepared, with clean towels laid to one side, and a huge bar of soap.

'There.' She tested the water, and motioned to him to undress. 'Get in while it is hot. I shall be back in a moment.'

Without a word he did so, but not without some reservations. This bright-eyed woman was not the same one who had spoken with him this very morning. His pulse quickened as the door opened and she came in again, and he saw she had discarded her surcoat and gown and wore nothing but a plain shift, which did very little to hide the curves and fullness of her breasts from his searching eyes.

He plunged himself beneath the hot water and came up gasping for air, and said harshly, 'Soap, woman! I smell of horses and men.'

'I am well aware of that, my husband.' Alisandre took a large bar of the herb soap that was made at Wynterfold and began to lather his chest. He sat immobile, watching her, the pale green eyes betraying no emotion at her touch. She lathered the soapsuds into his short hair, across the broad shoulders, her fingers slowly caressing the faint scars there and remembering, as he did, as she touched them.

'There. Is that better? Or am I not competent at these things? I am not accustomed to them, but it was something my mother always told me I should do for my husband. Attend to his every need, she said. Nothing is too trivial, or too exacting for you to do, if he needs it.'

'Do you hear me complaining, Kutti?' Rollo smiled, and the paleness of his eyes was suddenly like the bottom of a sea lagoon—tranquil—where one could laze at lease and forget the world. She was achieving her aim, Alisandre realised. She knelt over him, and he sat up so that she could soap his back. Water splashed over the front of her shift without her noticing it, but Rollo did, and a tight knot formed in his stomach as he saw the outline of her breasts against the thin material. He wanted to grasp her and pull her into the tub with him. Swallowing hard, he reached out and began to unfasten the ribbons which secured her hair. She looked at him questioningly, but he said nothing, and she continued with what she was doing.

Before she had finished the lathering, her hair was loose about her shoulders, so long now that it was below her waist.

'Never cut these magnificent tresses, Kutti.' He leaned forward and buried his face in the depths of the loose hair. It smelled of lemon balm and herbs, fresh and clean.

'Only if I lose you.' She sat back on her heels and looked at him, her face strangely serene. 'If—If anything should ever happen to you, I shall shear this head like the coat of a sheep.'

'Why?'

'So that no other man will ever see me as you have. No man will ever touch my hair and take pleasure in that touch. I belong to you and to no other. Will you never accept that?'

'How have I done otherwise?' He knew why she asked, and sought for an answer that would not spoil what she had conjured up this evening for them both.

'You have neglected me,' she declared in all innocence, and his face tightened.

'I? Have neglected you? Woman, I have scarcely seen you these past two days!'

'And whose fault is that? You tell me I am mistress here, that I must take control, and that I have done. And where have you been? Instead of resting and regaining your strength, you have been riding, practising at the quintain with your men, drinking with them at night. You reek of wine when you come to bed, exactly as you do now!' Alisandre sprang to her feet, her eyes blazing. 'Who has been neglecting whom, my lord? Do I not anticipate your every wish? Is the food not to your liking? Do you not have enough?'

'Kutti, take care . . .'

'Or what? I shall be on the wrong end of the Lord of Darkness's unpleasant tongue? How many times has that happened already? I am not afraid of your temper or your moods. Now, have you finished with me? May I go?'

'If the task was so unpleasant, why did you perform it in the first place?' Rollo asked, grim-faced as he climbed from the tub and wound a towel round himself.

'Because it pleased me to do so.' She gave a wicked grin and turned towards the door. 'Supper is ready, if it pleases my lord to eat.'

She heard him mutter under his breath, as she ran to the bed and pulled from it the robe of saffron silk embroidered with gold thread. With sudden boldness she rubbed sweet-smelling salve into her skin before slipping into the robe and fastening it with a single loop across her breasts. It was cold against her nakedness, and she shivered. She thrust her feet into pointed slippers of rich golden leather, and waited for Rollo to emerge.

With only the towel about him, he came expecting to climb into bed, she suspected, even though she had told him there was food prepared. He had seen none when he came, but now, thanks to the servants' diligence—and silence—a feast awaited him. Would he remember, she asked herself, as he stood looking at the table that had been arranged before the fire. Two stools had been drawn up beside it, an embroidered tapestry thrown down alongside the hearth. On the table were chicken and wild boar, freshly-made cheese and butter, together with bread baked that morning in the kitchen ovens. An abundance of wine, he noticed, and two goblets, and a smile began to curve about the hard line of his mouth. As though he needed the inducement of heady wine!

'My lord is pleased by my humble offering?' Alisandre asked with a meekness of tone that did not go with the light flickering in her eyes.

In two long strides he had crossed the space between them and caught her against his chest, one hand entangled in her hair to tug back her head, and stared down into her softly glowing cheeks. 'You are no servant, Kutti, no harem woman! Nor will I have you behave like one.'

'My lord thought himself neglected . . .' It was hard to keep up the pretence of servitude when he looked at her in that way, and as her voice wavered, his pale eyes gleamed with mockery.

'Do something about it then, wench.'

She gasped at the taunt, and tried to pull free of him, but he, with a laugh, took her mouth, bruising it with a ferocity she had not known for many months. For a moment she fought him, reluctant to concede defeat even though surrender was what she had anticipated throughout the whole day, but there was no mercy in his kisses. He sought to dominate her, and he succeeded.

'Rollo...' She sank against him, drained and spent. 'The food!' He ignored her, and her fingers lost themselves in the thatch of thick black hair as he opened her robe and his hands began to explore her body. This was not how she had intended it to be. They were to have eaten together, consumed the wine, and then made love, but with Rollo, nothing was ever as it should be—and she thanked God for it! He parted her lips with kisses that sent her pulse racing, and she felt as if the ground moved beneath her feet.

'Do not seek to tame me, Kutti,' he whispered against her cheek. 'I am yours. Let that be enough.'

'I do not want to tame you,' she whispered, laying her own lips against his cheek first and then against one shoulder, where the marks of torture stood out clearly against the bronzed skin. 'I suspect you have long claws, and will escape from any cage meant to hold you. Rather, I seek to know, and to learn—to please.'

'Have you not done so already?' Rollo murmured.

She gave a low moan, pressing herself more tightly against him as his caresses grew more persistent. He slipped the robe from one shoulder, and followed it as it fell away to the upward tilt of her breast. His fingers stroked and teased, and then he bent his head and gently kissed the place where his fingers had been. Alisandre's legs turned to water at the sensation that engulfed her.

'You have given me what you have never given another man, Kutti,' Rollo whispered. 'The greatest treasure you possess—your love.'

With trembling fingers she reached for the fastening of the robe, but it was he who swept it open, sliding his hand around her back, then down over slim buttocks, pressing her hard against him so that she felt his own desire.

'No tomorrows, my love. Your own words. Let it be like that for us now,' she pleaded.

With an oath, he tore away the robe and, lifting her in his arms, laid her down on the softness of the coverlet, pulling away the towel. He lost himself in the exploration of her mouth until she groaned and clung to him, trembling like an aspen, telling him that her need was as great as his.

Then she drew back, her loose hair a cloud of fire streaming across the bolster, her body crying out for him as it had done for these past three nights. 'Satisfy your hunger, my husband. And mine,' she begged.

'So I was right. It is in you, too. What game have we been playing, Kutti?'

'I don't know, but it frightened me. I am here—I always shall be. Do not ignore me again, I beg you. I ache for you to hold me, to touch me. Take me, please...'

'Slowly. Gently,' Rollo murmured. 'Such moments should never be rushed.'

Alisandre closed her eyes, giving herself up completely to the sheer ecstasy of his touch, the sensations of fire running up and down her limbs as first his hands and then his mouth continued to move over her body. Seeking, exciting, dominating her with the skill of his lovemaking. Her hands clutched at his shoulders as he moved over her, his hard, muscular body pressing hers into the mattress, trembling, eager... She could hear herself gasping for breath as she returned kiss for kiss, caress for caress, allowing herself to be drawn over the threshold of that other world where nothing existed but the two of them. The wave carried her on and on into a sea of passion and fervour which, as it began to recede, left her drained... trembling still... fulfilled.

She became aware of Rollo drawing away from her. On bare feet he moved to the door, and stood for a moment listening, before returning to her. 'I thought I heard a cry. Our son, perhaps?'

'I am weaning him on solid food now, and have been for the past month, so that he should not wake on a night such as this,' she returned, her eyes alight with wicked lights.

He stretched out beside her and gathered her to him again, content in the afterglow of their love. If only it could always be like this, but there were things to be done that he could not discuss or share with her, even though he dearly longed to. She had given him a chance to lay aside his sword for a few weeks or months, but it mattered not so long as he could spend them with her in such peace. To spend the remainder of his days lost in this new wonder which had arrived in his life, to confound and confuse him. It was there, and could not be denied. Ignored—as he must ignore it soon—but never denied!

'Kiss me, Kutti,' he ordered, and she looked at him in surprise. His fingers, light as a summer's breeze, moved slowly over her skin to reawaken the embers

of the fire which had consumed her so completely.
'Kiss me as you did at Shah'mat. Is that not where
we are now?' He was remembering that night, when
she had recovered part of her memory and he had
held her in his arms and shown her such gentleness
as she as never known in him before.

Hesitantly she slipped her arms about his neck and
brought his dark head down to hers. Love made her
bold, seeking to satisfy him as he had her. How strange
his eyes were, she thought, as she arched her body
upwards against his. They looked at her, yet were
without expression—as if part of him had closed a
door and shut her out. Yet his fingers burned her skin
as they plundered her body. She fell back on the
pillows, bringing him down over her.

The explosion of passion came without warning.
Even as their lips clung, he parted her thighs and entered her again, instantly arousing the same sensation
of fire throughout her body. Then he began to move
slowly inside her, exciting her to such a pitch that she
thought she would scream aloud if he did not finish
it. His hands were never still. There was no part of
her body that he did not touch, explore, devastate with
them. The fierce pressure of his mouth on hers
silenced her cries as his slow thrusting continued to
prolong her desire to be satisfied.

And then his movements quickened. The wave
swept her before it, held her for a moment on the
peak of heaven's mountain, and then thrust her down
upon a blissful shore of contentment. If she lost him,
at least she had glimpsed paradise, she thought, as
she drifted into sleep.

CHAPTER FIVE

THE FOLLOWING three days were the happiest Alisandre had known since her return to Wynterfold. Rollo totally abandoned the quintain and spent every moment with her. They spent long hours together in the solar, before a blazing fire, with Jarl playing at their feet. Talking little, content to be in each other's arms, a family together. These moments would comfort her when he was away, she thought, as she nestled against him.

They hunted together, and she watched him fly the short-winged goshawk he had acquired. Something must have shown on her face, for the next day he gave her the bird for her very own. Had he offered her a chest of jewels instead, she would still have chosen the bright-eyed goshawk, and was so delighted with his gift that she flung her arms round his neck and soundly kissed him before everyone.

'You will have to behave yourself when your cousin returns!' he told her.

'Will I?' Alisandre looked up at him saucily. 'Why, pray? I am mistress here, am I not, and I shall behave as I please. And if I choose to kiss you in the middle of the Great Hall, I shall. What harm is there in it? I am your wife, not some serving-wench you have taken a fancy to. If that happened, I suppose you would hide in one of the alcoves so that no one could see you. Would you have me do the same...' She broke off as Rollo's eyes flashed angrily. 'Oh, I didn't mean! Of course I know you wouldn't look at another woman—you have no need. I mean . . . Oh, dear!'

She ran from his presence with his laughter ringing in her ears. She was still so innocent that he could not stay cross with her for long. Her openness had always appealed to him, her complete lack of guile. He hoped she would never change.

'Rollo, I have been through the accounts ledgers with Ponsford, and although Wynterfold is self-sufficient and in good repair, it would appear that my cousin has been rather liberal with her spending. I know it has all been for the good, but...'

'There is no money in the coffers. I did not expect there to be. Cousin Margaret and her comforts come first, Wynterfold second. Only, I suspect, because it might one day be useful to Prince John. Everything else, and everyone, has to fend for itself,' Rollo responded. 'Is it so hard to ask me for what you want? This is your home, and I am well pleased at the way you are running things now. You shall have whatever you need.'

'I shall use it wisely,' she promised.

'I shall expect an accounting for every coin,' he said, and then his face broke into a smile at the indignation rising in her expression. 'Nay, Kutti, all I have is yours—except for one coffer, which will go towards ransoming the king of England. Tomorrow we shall ride to Winchester together. Do you think Ponsford could sit a horse for that distance? He has a keen eye, and knows a fair price.'

He broke off and turned, his eyes sweeping towards the main entrance. A horseman was bearing down on them at a fast pace.

'Stand fast,' Rollo ordered. 'Only Siward rides like that.'

Horse and rider were one as the enormous gelding came galloping through into the protection of the thick encircling wall without faltering in its magnificent stride.

'I think perhaps we may have to postpone our trip, Kutti. Siward does not ride an animal into the ground for no reason,' he murmured, striding to greet the breathless Norseman who came sliding from the back of his lathered horse to be warmly hugged and slapped soundly on the shoulders.

'You have ridden like the wind, Siward. What news do you bring? Is Richard free?'

'Nay, my lord, he still languishes in some Austrian prison, but the word has gone out among the people, and even the most ordinary peasant has come forward to offer a coin towards his ransom. It would have gladdened your heart to see how they came out into the streets of London, calling out Richard's name. Prince John's departure was hardly noticed. It was all Richard: Richard the Lion-Heart: the true king!'

'It does gladden my heart. As long as we can keep John's greedy hands off the money when it is collected and get it safely to France, to Queen Eleanor, then Richard will be freed, and I pray I am there the day John kneels to pay homage to his brother.'

'Prince John goes to France himself. He is on his way to the coast now, which is why I rode like Satan's hounds to return.'

'My message was delivered?' Rollo asked, lowering his voice so that his wife was only just able to hear the words.

'It was. I received no written message in return. I was told to tell you "to do whatever has to be done, in the name of the true king."'

Alisandre saw Rollo's shoulders stiffen. She was dying of curiosity, but knew better than to question him directly. 'Come inside,' she urged the two men. 'It is too cold to stand and talk out here. I want to hear all about London, Siward. I was only six the last time I went there with my parents.'

'You are right, my lady, we cannot stand here—nor do I have time, regretfully, to answer all your questions. Prince John and Lady Margaret are half a day behind me. They are coming here. It was her idea... He will stay overnight and continue on to the coast tomorrow. I thought you would welcome advance warning.'

'Prince John here?' Alisandre gasped. 'That's impossible! How many are with him?'

'Around fifty courtiers, men and women, and the same amount of men at arms,' Siward said with an apologetic smile.

'We have just enough provisions perhaps,' she muttered to herself as she picked up her skirts and fled into the house, calling for Ponsford and the servants to attend her at once.

'It will be good to take a close look at the enemy, Siward,' Rollo remarked as they turned and followed.

'You did not tell me I was to meet such a distinguished person,' the Norseman said, wishing he could tell what went on behind that inscrutable face.

Rollo's eyes had darkened to the colour of a storm-tossed sea, and his thoughts were locked away in their depths—for himself alone. 'You were well received?' He was sure Siward would be surprised to discover that the man he had gone to see was none other than the Regent of England himself, Walter de Coutances, Archbishop of Rouen, a Cornishman by birth to whom Richard had given full powers during his absence. *He* would not be dislodged from his post or sent scurrying out of the country as others had been. And now he would know of Rollo's loyalty, and the letter accompanying his own from the Dowager Queen Eleanor would explain the mission that had brought him back to England.

'I had only to speak your name, as you bade me. You are well thought of, my lord, and your help appreciated. But I was to impress upon you that there are spies and traitors everywhere—that you can trust no one. You must do whatever has to be done without confiding in another living soul.'

'I had already accepted that,' Rollo said. Then his face cleared, and he laid an affectionate arm about the man's shoulders. 'Let us go and warm ourselves with some wine, and talk in the solar. It will probably be the only place the women do not invade. I plan to leave for France as soon as the weather improves, and I must be sure that all will be well here until I return.'

'So soon?' Siward queried.

'There is much to be done at Verduse. I can see by your face that you do not approve of the rebuilding,' Rollo said. 'Neither does Alisandre, but my decision is made. One day soon I hope to be able to explain all. Come, let us talk . . .'

'I have always had a soft place in my heart for Wynterfold,' John, Count of Mortain, declared, and all eyes went directly to the woman who stood at his side. It was in many minds that it was Margaret de Greville-Wynter that drew him here, not anything to do with the house. How would it be now that another ruled in her place, an ally of King Richard, she and her Norman husband both?

He was nothing like his brother, was the first impression which came into Alisandre's mind as she and Rollo greeted him just after four that afternoon. The Guard proudly flanked the royal personage and escorted him into the Great Hall, which in a short while had been miraculously transformed for their eminent guest.

Where Richard was tall, a majestic figure, his younger brother was of medium build, with very ordinary features that did not inspire any feeling of awe in her. He could be a calculating, if not ruthless man, she suspected, noticing how his dark brown eyes constantly surveyed all about him, silently assessing the worth of his surroundings. For the ransom of his brother, or his own personal coffers? And a vain one, by his colourful apparel.

Margaret looked equally impressive in burgundy velvet, about her throat a necklace of rubies, each one of the seven stones against the whiteness of her skin as large as that which adorned John's cloak. Instinctively Alisandre knew whence it had come, and she knew a moment of intense disquiet. Was she wrong about her cousin? Because of her help, and her concern for Wynterfold during Alisandre's absence, was she being blinded to the true nature of this woman?

Rollo had disliked her on sight. Siward disliked her, too, and she trusted both their reactions, and yet in her heart she could not bring herself to think badly of Margaret. A woman in love was often tempted to go against her true self, to surrender herself to the man she loved, and face the consequences undaunted. Was that not what she herself had done? If Prince John was Margaret's lover, where was the harm? He had a wife, but she had heard that the marriage was not happy, and men always took mistresses when their wives bored them. Rollo's absence in France would trouble her, not because she thought he might take a mistress, but because she knew he would sorely need her, as she needed him. Very conscious of the looks which came her way, she tried to lose herself in the making of conversation, but found it somewhat difficult. Margaret's attention was for Prince John alone. By her own side, Roger Chabret was telling her of the court and how she must soon present herself and begin to meet people. Rollo was very quiet. She knew that Roger Chabret's attentions to her were beginning to annoy him by the scowl that came to his face whenever he looked at the young man. He was harmless, she decided. In love with Margaret and totally under her spell, but harmless, even though he did lean too close to herself at times, forcing her to move away.

She had never entertained on such a grand scale before, and was pleased with her efforts and those of the servants who had worked extremely hard to make it a success for her. Everyone seemed to have enormous thirsts, even the women, who appeared to find it amusing to try and keep up with the consumption of their companions. She found the sight revolting. Thirstiest and hungriest of all was Prince John, who had even turned his attention away from Margaret, for the first time since their arrival, she noticed, to give the food before him his most avid concentration. And *this* was to take the place of Richard Coeur-de-Lion? It was an appalling thought!

Siward, standing behind Rollo's chair, bent to refill her goblet, waving aside the servant who had come to do so. 'His brains are in his stomach, my lady. He will never rule England,' he whispered in her ear, as if he had read her thoughts, and she could not control the involuntary laughter which came bubbling to her lips. Rollo's head came around like a whiplash to see the cause of her mirth and the eyes considering the two of them narrowed suddenly to pale glittering chips of green ice as Margaret leaned across to him and laid a hand over his arm.

'Alisandre is so lucky to have two men who dote on her, my lord. Your man acts the lady's maid well, does he not? So meek and docile when he is with her. On the road with me, he was a churlish boor, scarcely able to find a word of conversation. I was glad when he left us early. I gather he rushed back here to tell my cousin of the prince's coming. How thoughtful.'

Rollo turned, and looked into the beautiful face and the innocent smile masking it. 'He merely anticipated your sending a messenger, my lady. You were about to do so when he left, I am sure. You would not have wanted Alisandre to be embarrassed by an unexpected guest of such importance would you?' The cold eyes challenged her, told her that he knew this was exactly what she had intended should happen. Thanks to Siward, it had not. But damn it, he thought, moving his arm from beneath the long fingers, did Siward have to display his devotion to Alisandre so openly?

He realised that Alisandre was staring at him, and she had gone very pale as she sensed some inner torment inside him. He tried to force a smile to his face, but failed. The blackness was descending further on him with every minute. He could not shrug it off, and despaired of ever fully trusting to the instincts of his heart again. He had tried—God knows, he had tried—but the wounds Lisette had inflicted had been opened once again to sear his soul and blacken his mood. He needed something to divert him.

Alisandre's apprehension that something was wrong heightened as Rollo rose slowly to his feet, motioning with a wave of his hand for empty goblets to be filled. His bleak gaze swept the entire hall, silently challenging those who sat watching him, each with their own thoughts about this strange enigma who had invaded their midst.

'My Lord Prince, ladies, fellow brothers in arms, I give you a toast.' He raised his goblet high, head thrown back, one hand on his hip; an arrogant stance, which made Prince John purse his lips. 'Let us all drink to the safe return of Richard Coeur-de-Lion, king of England.' Rollo's voice rang out through the Great Hall. Reaction was varied: without hesitation, Rollo's Guard, Alisandre and Rollo himself drank, together with a few of the guests; others waited, their eyes riveted on the stony face of Prince John. There was a sigh of relief as he raised his goblet, and then drained it. Rollo bowed in his direction, considering the tight lips and gleam of anger in the eyes that stared back at him.

'More wine,' Rollo ordered. 'And let us drink another toast. Long life to John, Count of Mortain, who has guarded his brother's throne so diligently these past years. May God smile on his efforts to raise the ransom to free the king and bring him speedily back to England and his people.'

This toast was accepted quickly, and the hubbub of conversation that filled the room as Rollo sat down again helped to ease the mounting tension. At a signal from Rollo, a large chest was brought and deposited before the long table where John sat, and the lid opened. There were gasps and exclamations of surprise as the contents—gold and silver coins, plates and goblets—were exposed. 'This is my contribution towards the ransom of King Richard,' he declared proudly.

'You put us all to shame with such generosity, but it is no more than I would expect from one so close to my brother as you are, my lord.' John's smile took the edge from his words, but there were many who did not miss the underlying tones of displeasure. 'I shall be honoured to take charge of it and deliver it into safe hands.'

'I would not dream of putting Your Highness to any trouble. I shall be on my way to the court of Queen Eleanor within a very short time, and I shall deliver this small token personally. Of course, if anyone else cares to add to it, I shall be glad to convey any additional contributions.'

The prince's face darkened. 'The coast road is a dangerous one, my lord. Take care with such a valuable burden. Should you change your mind, you may leave the chest with Roger Chabret, who will personally guard it until it is in safe hands.'

Yours, Rollo thought, as he smiled without answering.

'The Lord of Darkness has a Guard of ferocious fighters, Your Highness.' Margaret, who had been watching the battle of wills with growing interest, decided to take a hand and push the two contestants a little further. 'I very much doubt if there is a single

knight in the realm who can best them. Why should
we not enjoy the spectacle of skilled men testing their
strength against each other? In friendly combat, of
course.'

'Why not? But it will be a short spectacle,' the
prince returned, trying not to show his sudden en-
thusiasm. What a witch this woman was! If Rollo were
killed before everyone, it would look like an accident,
and he himself would proclaim it so and absolve the
victor from all blame. That left only the Lady
Alisandre, and she was no more than a child who
could easily be dealt with. He would place her under
his protection, marry her off to some wealthy knight
who would pay handsomely for her charms, and
return Wynterfold to his mistress. He surveyed the
sea of faces in front of him, already growing ani-
mated at the prospect of some sport. Whatever happened, he knew he had enough men to overcome the
few that might side with Lady Alisandre if her
husband was hurt or killed. And there were always
those paid by Margaret, who were ranged inconspicu-
ously around the room. This Duke of Aquitaine must
pay for interfering in matters which were none of his
business!

'You and your men may withdraw and prepare
yourselves. In one hour, we shall discover who is the
most skilled fighting man in this room.'

'I wish to be alone,' Rollo said, glowering at the young
squire who continued to linger in his apartment after
he had been dismissed. Rising to his feet, he went to

the window and opened the shutters. A blast of cold air blowing through one of the many cracks beside the window hit him full in the face, but he did not move back. The heat of the Great Hall, the food and wine, had all helped to dull his senses and slow his reactions, and he needed a clear head to be at his best against Prince John's contestants. He did not doubt that some of them would be very good.

Before he reached the end of the staircase, he knew by the sounds of laughter and the loud voices that the spectacle was going to be appreciated. He froze in the shadows, unseen by the couple who were talking a few feet away, melting back into the darkness of a recess in the wall as the woman threw back her head and laughed at a comment by her companion, and he heard his wife's name clearly mentioned.

'Did you not notice the one behind Lady Alisandre's chair? The blond one with the scarred face?'

'I'd not want his ugliness on a pillow beside me,' came the derisive retort.

'That kind of thing attracts some women. Perhaps she has discovered he has other—redeeming— qualities that make up for it. I swear I could feel him bristle if another man so much as looked at her, let alone touched her hand. I wonder if the Duke of Aquitaine is aware of how faithful his Guard are?' The man chuckled again as he escorted his companion back towards the Great Hall, unaware of how close he had come to sudden death.

Slowly Rollo overcame his anger and replaced the dagger in his belt. A brief glimpse of the man's face as he emerged into the light had stayed the deadliness of his hand, held back the violence of the temper about to be unleashed. He did not attack in the dark, from behind, tempting as the notion had been for one mad moment. Instead, he had printed the bearded face and thin hawk nose on his memory. If he did not have satisfaction tonight, he would exact it before he left these shores! Then as he stepped from the shadows, a figure totally clothed in black save for the silver bolt of split lightning embroidered on his overtunic, he saw his wife and Siward.

The accusation on Rollo's bleak features, illuminated by a wall torch, momentarily stunned Siward. Rollo could not think . . . But he did, Siward realised, as he had once before at Shah'mat, when he had seen them riding and laughing together, and his jealousy had planted venomous thoughts in his mind to torment him.

'You are neglecting our guests, woman.'

The harsh voice brought a flush of colour to Alisandre's cheeks. With great dignity, she stepped down to face her husband. 'Is the food not to your liking, or the wine, that you take your foul temper out on me?' Her voice shook at the shame she felt at being thus addressed before Siward.

'Your guests are obviously unimportant, if you linger and ignore them,' Rollo snapped.

She gasped at the unfair words, her own temper rising. 'I was attending to the needs of our son, which

I consider come before anyone, except you, my lord. Are our guests not important to *you*, that you come seeking me instead of entertaining them yourself?' she flashed, and the pale green eyes considering her narrowed angrily.

Slowly they travelled the whole length of her body. They missed no detail of her appearance. What was he looking for, Rollo wondered? Flushed cheeks from a stolen kiss? She had those, but from his curtness. A stray dishevelled lock of hair? Her skirts creased? He found nothing amiss.

She moved to one side to go past him. His hand snaked out and fastened over her wrist in such a painful grip that she winced in pain. Without a word, he propelled her into the Great Hall and sat her down beside him, her cheeks now flaming as many eyes turned to watch their entrance. He looked like an angry bear, and her embarrassment heightened as heads bent together as Siward followed them, to stand behind Rollo's chair—and those eyes turned again to watch his entrance and speculate and wait for confirmation.

CHAPTER SIX

'YOUR GUARD fight well, my lord.' Prince John turned in Rollo's direction. 'Now it is time to show us how the master conducts himself. Fitz-Hugh——' he nodded towards the hawk-nosed knight who had approached the table '—my unbeaten champion, will test your prowess.'

The man was strong, Rollo discovered the moment their blades clashed for the first time and he allowed his own weapon to be forced down to discover how much strength he would need to hold it fast. More than he had anticipated, he thought, disengaging at the very last moment and, neatly side-stepping the heavier, less nimble man, came round to attack from the left side.

'You will have to do better than that,' he mocked quietly, and there was a deadliness about the tone that warned Fitz-Hugh that this was no game. The accompanying glitter in the pale green eyes reminded him of a wild-cat about to strike. 'The last man who insulted my wife also died by my hand. Did you know Hugo de Greville-Wynter, my loud-mouthed friend?'

Fitz-Hugh did not try to deny his words. He was glad they had been overheard and brought about this confrontation, for they saved him the trouble of seeking the man out at a later date and inventing some excuse for killing him. 'I knew Hugo, my lord. I did not call him friend, however. His many—shall we say—peculiarities made it difficult for any real man to do that. You will not dispose of me as easily as you did him.'

'Shall I not?' The two-handed sword in Rollo's hand was a blur before Fitz-Hugh's eyes. Weaving, parrying, never still, the candlelight on the finely polished steel seared his vision until his eyes ached. An old Saracen trick, he recalled, which they had used many times in battle, near blinding their adversaries with the fierce glare of the sun on their shields and weapons that had been deliberately polished to a high sheen. He shook his head and backed away, Rollo forcing every step. He gained no advantage from his years of fighting. This man anticipated every move with unerring accuracy. It was uncanny—as though he could read minds!

'You can always yield, Fitz-Hugh! I'd enjoy hearing your tongue curl around an apology.' Rollo was without mercy. Several times he flashed a quick glance towards the top table where Siward stood watching him—close to where Alisandre sat, as though it were his God-given right to be so near to her! Yet had he himself not granted that concession? What was the matter with him? She was not at fault, yet he had done nothing but find fault with her all evening. When he told her she must be more reserved in her manner, she would understand how careful she must be and all would be well again between them. By morning, they would be laughing at his ridiculous jealousy! But first he would deal with Fitz-Hugh, so that no other man would be foolish enough to follow in his footsteps!

'You dare not kill me!' Fitz-Hugh flung the words at Rollo with false bravado. Had he not planned to kill him and make it look like an accident—a slip of his sword in the heat of the moment? Why could he not do the same? No one else knew of the enmity between them.

'Kill you—here—before Prince John, and have a knife in my back the moment I stepped outside? No, hawk-nose!' The derogatory name brought an expletive to the other man's lips. 'Not here. In the darkness outside, perhaps, or in the woods tomorrow when you leave. An arrow out of the sky may well bury itself in your chest, and you will fall from your horse without ever seeing the face of your attacker. Perhaps it will be me . . . perhaps not. Who knows?'

'You are a knight, a man of honour. Do you think, because I die, the talk will stop? You cannot hold back the truth, my Lord of Darkness, or whatever name you choose to call yourself. I am only one of many you will have to fight. Are you blind to what goes on about you, or, like the Infidel, have you grown used to sharing your women?'

With a snarl of rage, Rollo swung the huge broadsword in an enormous arc, the blade cutting down with great force towards the man's head. Fitz-Hugh blocked the stroke, which would have severed his head from his body, but only just, and was forced to his knees.

'So you are only a man like the rest of us. A vulnerable man who has been cuckolded by his wife! Why do you hesitate? Kill me—or are you afraid? Yes, I think you are! But of what? Of the truth that your wife with her innocent face and the man you set to protect her have been deceiving you? Or is it Prince John's wrath you fear, my lord? If you kill me now, you will have a dozen men on you before you can take a step, and your Guard will not be able to protect you. One of them will not want to try. With you dead...' Fitz-Hugh cried out as a booted foot in his stomach sent him rolling over backwards on to the floor. At the same time, Rollo's sword began to descend towards him.

From a far-off distance Rollo heard a cry. His name... Alisandre calling his name, and the madness slipped from him sufficiently for him to deflect the blow. Instead of Fitz-Hugh's head rolling across the rush-strewn floor, it was his sword.

He staggered back from the enormity of what he had almost done, fighting to control himself. Men were on their feet applauding him, he realised dazedly, and he sensed there had been many, from the smiling faces, who not only disliked the man at his feet but would have liked to see him dead. He could use men like that. At last he could see who was friend and who was foe. With a tight smile he acknowledged Prince John, who sat like a statue gazing at his fallen champion.

John had seen, as many had, the terrible look on Rollo's face as his weapon came up for the stroke and

had known he was about to kill him. For that he would
never be forgiven. He was the better man, he had
proved that, and he was Richard's ally. More—a
friend! John could not count any of the men and
women surrounding him tonight as friends. He did
not have his brother's personality, or his ability to
keep people at his side through friendship, not bribery.

Rollo turned to Alisandre, and sketched an elab-
orate bow in her direction before sheathing his sword.
'My lady, your timely intervention saved me from
bloodying my blade on an unworthy opponent. In the
heat of the moment...' The last words, although he
did not look at John, were meant for him alone.

'Bloodying your blade?' the prince repeated stonily.
'Are these contests not meant to be of the friendliest
nature only? Your lack of control is no excuse for
nearly killing one of my men, my Lord Duke.'

'Some men make enemies more easily than others,
Sire. Your man did not have the smell of a friend
about him,' came the dry retort, and heads turned
back to the prince to watch his reaction at the barbed
reply. At the same moment, Siward stepped back from
Alisandre so that he was directly between John and
the Duke of Aquitaine. The divisions were already
being made, Rollo realised, as he saw an alertness on
other faces too. In his estimation, there were over two
dozen men in the Great Hall who would even now go
against John if asked.

Margaret leaned forward to the man at her side, a
hand on his arm, and whispered in his ear. John
listened with impassive features. When he drew back,

he said coldly, 'Your apology is accepted. I commend you on your prowess, my lord. England has need of such men. However, I regret you consider my men to be enemies—a threat to you. What say you to a friendly engagement with one who could not possibly wish to do you harm, and against whom you can have no possible resentment?' With a smile, he indicated Siward. There was silence in the Hall.

What had John's devious mind concocted now? Rollo wondered. To pit him against a man with whom he trained daily, had taught everything he knew in the art of warfare . . . Now he knew! John had set Fitz-Hugh against him with deliberate malice, using Alisandre to strike him at his weakest point! Siward was already coming forward with an unspoken question in his eyes to face him. What was he to do? Fight, and allow the last of his self-control to slip away as he considered what the prince would gain if he died? Or refuse, and have himself branded as a coward? Worse—a man who condoned an affair between his wife and a mere servant! He had no choice.

'My lord? I do not mind, if you are willing?' Siward's hand was upon his sword, but he had not yet drawn it as he considered the strangeness of Rollo's expression.

'Why not?' Rollo returned with a shrug of his shoulders. 'Let us show them how we fought for our king in the Holy Land. No man could best us then, nor can he now.'

For a moment they stared at each other in silence. Then, when it became obvious that Rollo had no in-

tention of making the first move, and out of the corner
of his eye he saw John deliberately smother a yawn
with a ringed hand, Siward pulled out his sword and
with a wild cry that filled the Hall, and sent the servants scuttling back into the shadows, he launched
himself at his lord.

Alisandre held her breath as she watched the encounter. Rollo's mood still bemused her. Had she not
intervened, she was sure he would have killed Fitz-
Hugh, but why? As far as she knew, the two men had
not met before this day. Now he was set against
Siward. She did not like it. For all the show of artistry
and amicability, she sensed a deeper reason for John's
suggestion. No man of Rollo's standing as a knight
liked to be beaten, or even one of Siward's.

Both Margaret and the prince were fascinated by
the encounter, and whispered often to each other.

'There are times when you are a fool, my lord!'
Siward said in a quiet, but very clear voice as his lips
almost touched Rollo's ear, and he froze, his pale eyes
glittering with anger that he dared speak so. 'I am still
only the man who rides at her side.'

How long had it been since that night at Shah'mat,
when he had left Alisandre there drinking with this
man, and he had questioned, then, Siward's friendship
with the woman not yet his wife. The smiles that
passed between them, the relationship which had developed from guardian and captive into loyal
champion and untouchable lady. He had not questioned Siward's words then; why should he now?

'My black thoughts will be the death of me, one day. When I saw you together...'

'Not then. Not now,' Siward said, this time in a fierce tone. 'Can you not see what is happening? One by one, with your suspicions and hatred, you will split us apart. We are your Guard. You are our lord. We must stay together, for the sake of us all!'

With a supreme effort, Rollo threw him back. Immediately Siward's sword came up to defend himself, but he needed only one glance into the green eyes to see that the glitter had diminished, and the tightness about the mouth was softening into an almost amused line.

'If you were any other man, I would kill you for those words,' came the almost imperceptible reply.

'If I was any other man, I would not have uttered them,' the Norseman said, still challenging.

Rollo's sword flashed upwards—not in a death blow, but in a salute of respect to the man who faced him, who had dared to call him a fool, and Siward's scarred face split into a relieved grin.

'Come and drink with me,' Rollo said, motioning him to the top table. 'Let us drink to the fool who dwells within this skin, and to the man brave enough to tell him so!'

'I am tired. I shall retire now. I thank you for your hospitality, my Lord Duke.' John rose to his feet, as a dozen or more goblets were filled and tossed back with fervour. He did not like what he saw, and he sought to bring back recalcitrant sheep into the fold by showing his displeasure. A few goblets were set down—others were not. Margaret rose at his side. She did not care who knew they were leaving together. She was immune to gossip.

'My dear, you look exhausted! Let me see you to your room,' said Margaret, bending to help Alisandre to her feet. She was exceedingly pale, and swayed slightly as she gained her feet. The older woman's face was filled with concern. 'You have carried off this whole evening admirably! I am so proud. I could not have done better.'

'You are too kind, cousin, but I fear the prince is not too pleased with my humble efforts,' Alisandre replied lamely. She did not care what he thought. The air reeked of conspiracy, Alisandre thought, as she descended the steps to where her husband stood, Siward and the other two Guards closely flanking him. Protecting him here, in her own house? she thought, again fired with the same indignation as when he had earlier insulted her. What did he expect to happen to him?

'Not pleased?' Margaret echoed. 'That is not the impression he gave me. When you know him a little better, you will discover he is not as flamboyant a character as his brother Richard. He has a quiet nature, and enjoys the simpler things of life.'

Rollo watched the two women out of sight before motioning the men present to make themselves comfortable, at the same time indicating by a nod of his head that the Guards should ensure they were not disturbed.

'My lords!' He fixed each of them in turn with a penetrating stare, and said in tones too low to carry beyond the table round which they sat, 'It is time we talked of how to raise the king's ransom—and how to get it safely out of England.'

It was several hours before the Great Hall became deserted. Rollo, as he did every night before he retired, made a tour of the keep, inspecting the new lines of defence he had instigated on the first day out of his sick-bed, and then went outside, with Siward close on his heels—as he always was at such times—to do the same with the sentry-posts. Satisfied that no unauthorised people were about, he returned to the house. He had drunk far too much, he realised, as he mounted the stairs to the bedroom. Alisandre would not forgive him if he further neglected her by falling asleep the minute he climbed into bed! The door immediately alongside him opened without warning, and his sword was half-way out of its scabbard before he saw and recognised Margaret, and allowed it to fall back into place.

'Oh, 'tis you, Lord Rollo . . .'

Brusquely he said, 'The hour is late, and I am tired.'

'I will not keep you more than a moment. I felt I should talk to you . . . about Alisandre.'

'My wife is none of your concern.' He tried to move past her, but she clung to his arm, and he felt her long nails digging into his skin through the material of his shirt.

'You should speak to her, my lord. I am sure she does not realise the speculation she has caused here tonight. I will approach her, if you think she would accept the reprimand better from another woman.'

'Alisandre has done nothing to be reprimanded for,' Rollo said harshly, and Margaret smiled in the darkness.

'Of course not! Then perhaps it would be more appropriate to speak to Siward? It is obvious that he worships Alisandre—which is not her fault, of course. These things happen. But the way his eyes follow her! I had a puppy like that, once, a sweet little creature, but it became too demanding. You obviously do not fear that. He is a trusted vassal, or you would not give Alisandre into his care. Others may not understand your apparent lack of concern. It is, after all, a common occurrence for wives to take lovers, and husbands, mistresses!'

'Alisandre has taken no lover, nor will she while I live,' Rollo snapped, furious that this woman had revived the subject.

'I could be of help, if you would allow it,' Margaret continued, again blocking his path. 'Especially as you are soon to return to France. Alisandre must be left in the care of someone older, and wiser in the ways of men. Since she is my cousin, I feel I should protect her...'

'You!' he sneered. 'And what is it you want in return for this solicitous help? You do want something, don't you, Lady Margaret?'

'How perceptive you are, my lord! I want the protection of your name while you are away; or, rather, that of your Guard. You could make it known that I...'

'If I am sure of anything, my lady, it is that you are well able to take care of yourself,' Rollo answered with a curtness that made her want to slap the mocking smile from his face. For every insult he delivered, he would pay dearly!

'It seems I must remind you that my brother is dead because of you! If I still had the protection of his name, I would not need yours. But I do not, and I fear for my future. If—If a certain person should tire of me, I might be married to some oafish knight and have no say in the matter. I no longer have Wynterfold, and that was important to him. It is the least you can do for me, my lord.'

'I shall—consider it.' His answer was a reluctant one and she knew it, but it was sufficient for the moment.

'You will not regret it. I shall be like a sister to Alisandre. No man will come near to her when you are gone. And I shall show you my gratitude, if you wish? To feel safe and secure again, I could be very, very grateful, my lord.'

Before Rollo realised her intentions, she had drawn his face down to hers and locked her mouth on his. He stiffened with shock, but did not move as she had expected. His hands fastened over her shoulders as though to push her back, but instead they tightened over her soft, cool skin and she was pulled against his broad chest. A wave of exhilaration swept through her. He was a mere man, after all, in need of a woman, not a child like Alisandre! Reaching up, she loosened one of his hands and brought it down to cup the fullness of one breast, pressing herself against him in a way she had always found aroused other men. From the deepness of his throat she heard a noise, and horrified, realised that it was laughter. He dared . . . !

She tried to free herself, but he held her fast, encircling her waist with one arm, while his fingers explored the body she had offered to him. She squirmed in indignation and rage, helpless to prevent his doing as he pleased. The ruthless pressure of his mouth muffled the insulting words that rose to her lips, and she was forced to endure a kiss that roused her as no other before. For years she had sought a man to satisfy her appetite, and had known only disappointment with each new lover. Until this man . . . !

As Rollo felt the change in her: the eagerness in the lips which no longer resisted his, the undulating movements of her body against his, his hands abruptly fell away from her, and he stepped back.

'Rollo, you and I . . .' Margaret whispered. 'At last, a real man!'

'Who is eager for the bed of his wife, not that of a prince's whore! Alisandre has no need of your company, my lady, nor you of my protection. Get you gone from this house by the time I return from France, or I shall throw you out!' He broke off as a door somewhere slammed, and frowned when he realised that only the room he shared with Alisandre was ahead. Margaret was pushed to one side, and her curses followed him the length of the corridor.

The bedroom was in darkness, except for a single candle burning beside the bed. That was empty. Where was Alisandre? In the nursery, with Jarl? Rollo was about to turn on his heel, when the sound of sobbing reached his ears. With an oath, he strode to the curtain across the small doorway leading to the antechamber and wrenched it open. Huddled upon the single bed there, was his wife. One look at the tearful features that came up to confront him, and the silent condemnation in the blue eyes swimming with tears yet unshed, told him who had been in the corridor—and that she had witnessed Margaret in his arms.

'Kutti, it was nothing!' Full of remorse, he threw himself down on the edge of the bed, but when he tried to gather her into his arms, to comfort her, as he explained what had taken place, she drew away, and struck out at the hands which tried to touch her.

'Go away. Go back to her!' The bitterness in her voice shocked him.

'Foolish child, what did you think you saw?' he challenged her.

'You, holding Margaret, kissing her as—as you kiss me!'

'No!' he snapped, barely able to contain his anger that she could think such a thing. 'I was teaching her that not all men are susceptible to a woman's smile, or the little morsels of attention she throws down. As some are.'

'You talk in riddles!' She despised the weakness in her, the love that had reduced her to tears. She should have been strong, and faced him with the accusation without flinching. The evidence of her own eyes could not be denied. He was tiring of her... and her cousin was only the first to attract him. And he pretended to dislike her! Yet, when she had heard him approaching, she had fled into this tiny room in an attempt to hide herself from him, and from the fear she suddenly felt in her heart. 'Did you have to—to amuse yourself beneath my roof? Could you not have gone down to the village if you needed a—a diversion?'

'*Your* roof, Kutti!' Rollo's features became bleak at her outburst. What madness had overcome her that she could even consider he would so much as look at another woman, let alone touch one in that way. 'This may be your house, but I am still master here.' *Your* master too, he almost added, but stopped himself in time. 'Come to bed and let me explain?'

'No, I don't want to listen to any more excuses, Rollo. I shall stay here. Alone.' Alisandre returned defiantly.

'Damn you!' he thundered, reaching for her. 'You are my wife, and you will obey me. Excuses! You dare to throw those words in my face! It is time I reminded you that I am your master as well as your husband!'

Alisandre gave a cry of alarm, as she was swept up in his arms and carried back into the other room and dumped unceremoniously on the bed. Rollo towered over her, his face black as thunder, hands on hips, and she shrank from the fury she could feel in him.

'I saw you... You cannot deny it!' Could he not understand the terrible hurt she felt?

'I do not.' She gasped as if he had struck her, and withdrew to the far side of the bed, clutching at the front of her robe with nerveless fingers. 'She was waiting for me... A favour was required. She needs the protection of my name while I am away. She fears that Prince John is tiring of her and intends to marry her off to some aged knight who will use her for breeding.'

'And you gave it to her. I saw the way she rewarded you,' she whispered. 'What else did she offer, my lord?'

'You try my patience too far, Kutti!' Rollo forced down an urge to grab her and shake her until she came to her senses. With narrowed gaze he considered the abject figure on the bed, and a sardonic twist deepened his mouth. 'She offered her services as your—companion. Like many others tonight, she thinks you are too free with your smiles where a certain man is concerned. There are some who are thinking he has become more than a bodyguard.' He had not intended to throw the words at her with such force behind them. He had not intended they should be uttered at all tonight, but she had angered him beyond reason.

'You... A man...Siward!' Alisandre gasped. 'Are you mad? What mists obscure your vision now, my lord? This is not the first time you have so unjustly

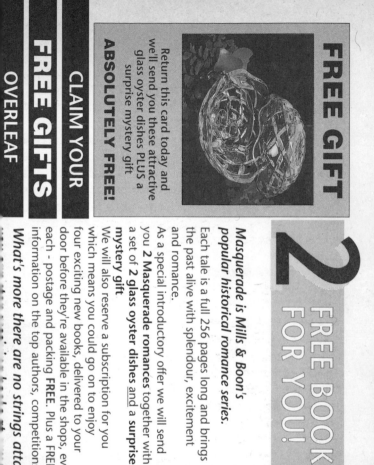

EXTRA BONUS

We all love surprises, so as well as the FREE books and glass oyster dishes, here's an intriguing mystery gift especially for you, no clues - send off today!

FREE BOOKS CERTIFICATE

Yes, please send me 2 FREE selected with my FREE oyster dishes and mystery gift and reserve a subscription for me. If I decide to subscribe I shall receive 4 new Masquerade titles every two months for £7.00, postage and packing FREE. If I decide not to subscribe I shall write to you within 10 days. The FREE gifts are mine to keep in any case. I understand that I can cancel or suspend my subscription at any time simply by writing to you. *I am over 18 years of age.* 5A9M

Name _____

Address _____

_____ Postcode _____

Signature _____

SEND NO MONEY NOW - TAKE NO RISKS

Reader Service
FREEPOST
P.O. Box 236
Croydon
Surrey
CR9 9EL

suggested that. I cannot believe you have spoken such words to me.'

'Did I not find you closeted together on the stairs this evening? You were touching him,' Rollo said accusingly. 'I saw that!'

'I did but question him about his visit to London! How dare you suggest . . .' Understanding dawned on her face. She came up on to her knees with fire blazing out of her eyes. 'You accuse me of—of what? Of taking a lover? To cover what is happening between you and my cousin, perhaps? I am not Lisette, and you will do well to remember it. One man is sufficient for my needs. One husband. If I have not already proved that to you, you are a fool!'

She flinched as she saw his fists clench, but he did not raise them from his sides. They faced each other like strangers, neither about to give way.

'Lisette is dead—as you will be if I discover you have ever lied to me in this matter.' The deadliness in Rollo's tone told her that it was no idle threat. 'You will heed my words, Kutti and cease to distract a man who has been ordered to protect you. He is a soldier— a fighting man. Do not treat him as you would one of the milksops we have entertained here tonight, or your name will soon stink with the same infamy as that of your cousin Margaret, innocent or not!'

'That stench did not seem to bother you tonight, did it?' she flung back. 'You cannot condone what I saw by trying to destroy my friendship with Siward. He is a good man, respectful and courteous—more so than his lord, most of the time! If you are tired of

me, say so, and I shall never come to you at Verduse.
I shall remain here, and no one need know the real
reason.'

The expletive which broke from Rollo's lips made
her wince with is crudeness. Before she could move,
he had flung himself on the bed and seized her by the
shoulders. The coldness of his expression as he opened
her robe told her this would be an act of revenge for
her words and her suspicions, not the act of love that
had so often brought them both pleasure and satisfaction, and she struggled frantically against his efforts to dominate her.

'You need to be reminded whom you are married
to, Kutti!' His lips sought hers, but she managed to
turn her face away, and he buried them in her loose
hair. She heard the robe rip as she tried to hold it
together over her body, but it was torn away and his
hands sought her breasts. Even like this, her body
began to respond to his touch, and she sobbed with
anger and frustration. He drew back from her, and
for a brief moment before he veiled it, she saw great
pain in his eyes. 'I could make love to you now and
you would welcome it, no matter what you say, and
enjoy it!'

'I am your wife. It is your right.' She lay un-
moving, her eyes never leaving his face. Her lips were
tightly compressed, her half-naked body rigid beneath the hand which still caressed her skin.

'Share my bed willingly—or get out of my sight!'

Alisandre could not believe she had heard aright.
There was no anger behind the words, no flicker of

expression on the dark face looking down at her. The cruel ultimatum took her breath away. His jealousy would destroy them all! She needed to think, to clear her mind of all but a way to make her husband believe in her—and in the man he had chosen to be her protector. She had to go!

Rollo withdrew to the edge of the bed as she eased herself away from him, drawing the robe high about her shoulders. He could not believe she was leaving. He sat staring at the oak door long after she had quitted the room, her face ashen, lips trembling visibly. He had only to open his mouth and say one word—Stay!—but he could not utter it. He could not beg!

CHAPTER SEVEN

CAREFULLY Margaret eased open the door of Rollo's room and slipped inside, closing it behind her without a sound. The room screamed chaos. He lay face down across the bed, sound asleep. Crossing to the table, her keen gaze quickly found what she had come for—a small carved ivory box containing his seals. Inside, she found the one she had seen him use on letters and other correspondence. She would need it for less than a day to have it copied. By nightfall, it would be back where it belonged, and she would possess such power as she had never known before: the power to oust Alisandre from her position as mistress of Wynterfold, to control the Guard, as if the orders she gave came from Rollo himself! Who would know the difference when he was in France, and every piece of parchment bore his seal? It had come to her in the night, as she racked her brain, seeking some way to repay his insulting behaviour. In the light of day, she felt confident of the success of her plan.

A restless movement from the bed brought her wheeling round, a hand against her mouth in sudden fear, but Rollo had simply turned on his back, one arm now outflung upon the pillow where Alisandre should have been. Her face a twisted mask of hate, which she had showed to no one since the news of her brother's death had been brought to her by Roger Chabret, she turned towards the door. To linger might mean she would encounter Alisandre returning from the nursery, where the maid had said she spent the night. One slippered foot caught on Rollo's discarded tunic. She lifted it with her toe, about to toss it across the room, when a thought struck her. From the front of her robe she took a scented handkerchief, and dropped it to the floor, allowing the tunic to fall on top of it. Only she used that distinct aroma of musk, and Alisandre knew it. As did the servants.

Rollo's room was still partly in darkness, the shutters only slightly open. Gy was laying out clean clothes for his master, while the maid was picking those up from the floor. The table had been cleared, overturned objects righted, the pitcher and goblet taken away, but, even so, Alisandre's nose wrinkled at the distinct lingering odour of wine and stale air. Had she driven him to seek solace in more wine? Oh, why had she not stayed! The maid stiffened suddenly, snatched something from the floor, and thrust it into a pocket. Her face paled as she turned and realised that Alisandre had come into the room.

Alisandre asked her, 'What did you pick up?'

'Nothing, my lady...a piece of cloth,' the woman stuttered.

'Cloth? Let me see it.'

'It is soaked in wine, my lady. It was probably used to mop up some that was spilt.'

'You found it beneath my lord's clothes.' Alisandre held out her hand, wondering why the woman should lie over a triviality. It was not like her. 'Give it to me at once, do you hear? Thank you.'

A strange coldness settled over her as she looked towards her husband and watched him rousing himself from the depths of a deep sleep. She had refused to sleep with him. Margaret had not, but had he gone looking for her, deliberately sought her company, or had her cousin come to him of her own free will? Had they made an arrangement while he held her and kissed her? Dear heaven, what was she to believe? A kiss could be forgiven. He had hurt her, but a marriage such as they had was too precious to be wrecked over a stolen kiss. But this—to take another woman to his bed because his wife had denied him his rights!

'What the devil is going on, Kutti?' Rollo eased himself on the pillows, rubbing his stiff neck muscles. His soldier's instinct told him instantly that something was wrong, and his gaze raked the room.

'Nothing, my lord. I came to get dressed to go down to our guests, that is all,' Alisandre returned. 'The prince leaves as soon as he has partaken of some food. He wishes to make good time to the coast. We do not want to be deemed inhospitable by not being downstairs to see him depart, do we?'

'I can tell by your tone that I am still not forgiven. Dammit, Kutti, I will not stand this coldness between us one more day!'

'I am sure I do not understand what you mean.'

Rollo stared at her with narrowed gaze and she waited in a painful silence while he finished dressing and then they went downstairs to oversee the departure of the prince and their guests.

Alisandre was aware of her husband staring at her many times as she said her good-byes, a half-puzzled, questioning look on his face. The prince was lavish in his praise of the hospitality he had found once again at Wynterfold, and was quite amiable to them both, with no trace of the irritation or anger he had shown the previous evening in his manner as Alisandre curtsied low beside the main door. Rollo just managed a stiff, polite bow.

'I hear from the Lady Margaret that you are to leave us again soon, my lord, to return to France?'

'For a few months only. My estates there are in need of my attention.'

'Of course. Lady Margaret has mentioned your concern for them. She has also spoken of her concern for her young cousin, and I am inclined to agree with her. Lady Alisandre cannot be abandoned to this lonely place so soon after she has arrived back in England. I shall insist that, as soon as I hold court again, she must attend. I assure you she will be well received. I shall make it known that she is personally under my protection. You need have no fear for her wellbeing while you are absent.'

If Rollo had been apprehensive before about leaving Alisandre alone, now his worry was heightened by this declaration.

'You are too kind, Your Highness. However, I assure you, I have sufficient protection for her here,' he returned stiffly, uncaring if he annoyed his royal visitor.

'I shall not hear of a refusal. Lady Margaret will bring her to court the next time she attends. Ah, the lady comes at last. How is it that a beautiful woman can always keep a man waiting without expecting reproach?'

Margaret came down the stairs behind them enveloped in a fur cloak, which trailed across the rushes as she hurried apologetically towards the prince. 'Forgive me...' She extended a ringed hand, which John carried to his lips. She had been listening out of sight on the stairs for several minutes. 'Alisandre, my dear, I have decided to ride with Prince John to the coast. I have relatives near Christchurch whom I have not seen in many months, and this will be a perfect opportunity to see them again.' If she noticed the coldness of her cousin's greeting, the cheek which avoided her fleeting kiss, she did not show it. 'I shall not hurry back. I know you want to spend as much time as possible with your husband before he leaves. I was a little hurt when he suggested I should depart this morning, but I now realise what was in his mind. He is more romantic than one would think, Alisandre. The Lord of Darkness keeps his secrets well!'

'Why, cousin, you have no reason to run away on my account,' Alisandre returned with iced sweetness. The mist of deception was wiped from her eyes now, as she gazed into the other woman's eyes and saw amusement there, and more—satisfaction!

In a torment of mind, she lifted her eyes to Rollo's face. He was looking at Margaret with no flicker of expression.

'Look to your wife, my lord. I fear she is unwell!' John said, as Alisandre swayed unsteadily, and immediately Rollo's arm was about her waist.

She grew paler still, and clutched at his hand, while painful memories came crowding in on her. It would not be so easy to resolve their differences here at Wynterfold, she thought miserably, as Prince John turned to go, and she forced her stiff legs into motion to follow him and the woman who walked by his side. Rollo's hold tightened as he felt the weakness in her. She longed to put her head against his shoulder, and weep.

As if he read her thoughts, as they reached the door he bent and laid his lips against her loose hair. 'What have you planned for today, Kutti?'

'I—I intend to go to Winchester, but tomorrow, perhaps, if you . . .' His question had taken her aback. Her heart leapt unsteadily at the throatiness of his tone, the way his fingers slid beneath her surcoat to cup her breast.

'Then, for the rest of the day, you are mine. We shall have no interruptions. And we shall not discuss the madness which has infected us both these last hours.'

'I shall not detain you, Rollo. I am sure you have things to do, as I have.'

His arm fell away at her cold tone, but his fingers fastened over her arm, detaining her as she turned to leave. 'What is wrong with you, woman?' he demanded in an exasperated voice. 'If you do not stop this foolishness this instant, I shall leave for France before the week is out!'

The ultimatum stunned her, left her speechless for several minutes. 'If that is what you wish, then go.' The words fell from her lips like a death-knell. She fought for composure, yet even with bright tears brimming in her eyes, she still retained great dignity. 'How long do you intend to stay away? I realise that there is much work to be done at Verduse and how important its restoration is to you, but in a few months your son will be one year old. Will you come back for that special occasion?'

'Do you think anything could keep me away? Dammit, I go because I have to!' Rollo snapped. 'I shall be back, and I hope my absence will have brought you to your senses... and that I return to a wife, not to a wilful child who is incapable of recognising the truth when she hears it! You wrong me with your suspicions, Kutti, and well you know it. I ask your forgiveness, if what you saw distressed you.' The words did not come easily to him. He had never been very good at apologising, and in this case he did not see the need for it, but if it would heal the rift between them, he would have uttered the words on bended knee.

'My lord Rollo, have you a moment?' Siward asked. He had been standing to one side watching them for some while, sensing that an interruption would not be well received.

Rollo wheeled on him with a scowl, demanding curtly, 'Well?'

'There are some men here from the village asking for your judgement on the matter of a stolen pig. You heard the details some days ago and were to deliver your decision today. Shall I send them away? Until tomorrow, perhaps?'

'No, Siward, my lord will attend to the matter. Neither of us can neglect our duties,' Alisandre replied before Rollo could do so, and turned away to where the servants were still waiting patiently for her to join them. Not until she had reached the bedroom did she realise that she had not replied to his question. He had asked her forgiveness, and she had said nothing! Would he leave in anger, or stay?

Rollo came into the room the following evening to find her kneeling over the chest he was to take with him that contained clothes and personal effects. The desolation on her face tore at his heart and wrung words from his lips that he had been trying to say for days. 'I *have* to go, Kutti. I don't want to leave you.'

'Do you not? Lately you have given me the impression that you are bored with life here—and with me.'

'Exasperating female!' Rollo groaned. 'You try my patience to the limit. Bored with you? I have not yet begun to know you—nor you, me. To think I would want any other woman after you!'

It had meant nothing to him, Alisandre thought in bewilderment, not understanding how a man could make love to a woman without love in him. How could she believe he truly loved her? Yet if she did not, she knew she could lose him.

'Oh, Rollo...' She jumped to her feet and ran into his arms, unable to deny him a moment longer. 'This must not happen between us again. I have been so wretched!'

'It is no more than you deserve for such unjust accusations,' he chided, tilting back her head to take possession of her lips. She allowed the words to go unanswered, no longer caring what had happened with Margaret.

'I shall not neglect you again, my husband,' she whispered, laying a flushed cheek against his chest. She would not let him slip away from her again— ever.

'Good,' Rollo chuckled, so relieved that the tension between them had gone that he gave her a rough hug, which made her gasp.

'Take care, my love and come back safely to us.' Alisandre held Jarl towards his father, and Rollo gathered him against his mail-coated chest and soundly kissed him.

Fascinated by the silver and black coat of arms, the boy remained quiet as Rollo caught Alisandre's hand and drew her to him. 'I shall miss you, Kutti. Take care of yourself and our son until I return. I shall not linger a day longer than is necessary,' he vowed, pressing his mouth on hers in a brief passionate explosion of emotion that brought tears to her eyes.

'Rollo...' She turned her face into his halberk, and was still for a long moment until she had composed herself.

He took her mouth for a last time, and her legs trembled at the intenseness of feeling he imparted into that kiss. Slowly—very slowly—as if he, too, was taken aback by the depth of emotion she had drained from him, he put her from him and gave Jarl back into her arms.

'I wish you were taking more men with you,' she said, looking at the covered cart carrying the chest of money and his personal effects.

'In this way, we do not draw unnecessary attention to ourselves,' he assured her. His gaze flickered to Siward, who was standing a few paces behind Alisandre. 'Take good care of her, my friend.'

'As I would you, my lord,' came the quiet reply, and Rollo nodded. Never before had a parting affected him so deeply. If he did not leave now... Without another word, he wheeled his horse about and rode after his men.

CHAPTER EIGHT

AT FIRST, the days did not drag. There was not a moment when Alisandre did not occupy herself fully, so that when she climbed into bed at night she would fall asleep directly. But after a few weeks the daily routine, which she now managed so skilfully that few problems occurred to do with the house or the estate, began to bore her. She took to riding daily, or sometimes she would fly the short-winged goshawk Rollo had given her when she arrived at Wynterfold—always with Siward in attendance.

It was the nights that nearly drove her mad. During the day, she ate very little, and only Berta's insistence made her sit down and partake of something light. At night she ate alone in the solar, sometimes with Siward, when she could persuade him to remain. He was still the same quiet, respectful companion he had always been, but there was a distance between them that she did not understand. Perhaps he, too, had heard of Rollo's indiscretion? She knew that, if he had, he would never mention it, he was far too loyal.

'Ponsford and Siward are back, my lady, but they hardly filled a quarter of the list you gave them.'

Alisandre rose and stretched, and stood rubbing her stiff neck for several minutes before following the

142

maid out of the solar into the Great Hall, where Ponsford stood fidgeting with some papers, as he always did when he was nervous. Siward stood to one side of him, his back towards her, staring out through the open door into the courtyard. His arms were folded over his chest, and something about his stance told her of a certain unease in him, too.

'My lady, I did my best,' the steward began, as she appeared. She waved aside his protests, and held out her hand. In a miserable silence he returned to her the list of items she had asked him to bring from Winchester. Barely a quarter had been purchased, she saw, and lifted questioning eyes to him.

'No paltry excuses! This is the second time you have returned almost empty-handed. What do you do with your time?'

'My lady, I have done all that you asked, but the shops are near empty. The new tax is crippling honest men and women. The prince is mad to impose such a harsh levy on us all!'

'What the man is trying to tell you is that Prince John has decided at last to show the people of England how much he cares for his brother's plight,' Siward broke in with a humourless smile as he turned to her, 'by allowing them to raise the ransom to free him.'

'But is that not what we expected?' she returned, frowning slightly. 'Everyone must help if the full amount is to be raised. One hundred and fifty thousand marks is a staggering sum.'

'And most could be found in the prince's own coffers, if we could but get to them. He has imposed a levy on the rich, the poor and even the clergy. One-quarter. One-quarter,' he repeated slowly as Alisandre's eyes widened in disbelief, 'of everything owned. Money, chattels and jewellery! Winchester was like a dead place.' Siward shook his head in disbelief at what he had seen. 'Shops closed and shuttered, warehouses with their doors thrown wide open, but no fear of thieves stealing what was inside, for Prince John's men had left nothing. A quarter, he said, but they took what they liked and were not gentle in the taking. No one was exempt. I heard it told that even the wool from the backs of the sheep raised by the Cistèrcian monks had been taken!'

Alisandre stifled a gasp of horror. The pious clergy were almost always given preferential treatment when it came to the raising of taxes. The Cistercians in particular, for their charity work and the poverty in which the order chose to live, were always a special case. The wool they sold was their only way of raising money with which to support themselves.

'Plate, silver and gold has been taken from the monasteries to be melted down. In many cases, more than the amount due. It will make some of John's men wealthy beyond their dreams.'

'And make paupers of the people of England,' she whispered, to which he gave a grim nod. Her mind was already racing to find an idea that would save Rollo's precious possessions.

'You think as I do,' Siward said, watching the frown that puckered her brows. 'How to prevent the prince's men getting their hands on Lord Rollo's money. We have two days, perhaps three, before Roger Chabret and his men get here to collect their due.'

'He is acting under orders from Prince John, so you will do nothing to antagonise him,' she replied. 'We shall hide my lord's coffers. Not all—just two. And we shall draw up an accounting for Sir Roger to sign before he leaves. Anything at all, even the slightest article of little value.'

'My lord would be proud of you,' Siward said, rising to his feet. 'But I forgot. I have other news, which is also distressing—for you. Saladin is dead.'

For a moment the news stunned Alisandre, more so than the other she had just heard. Saladin! He had looked ill and tired when she had seen him in Jerusalem a short time before Jarl's birth. Dead! In the hearts of his people, such a great leader would never die. There would always be a place for him in hers. 'I am indeed sad at these tidings. Many will rejoice, for he was a formidable foe, but he was a good man—a just man. I shall pray for his soul tonight.'

'How strange for a Christian to pray for a Muslim,' Siward said quietly.

'We are all one in the sight of God. Oh, there is something else. With all this news, it went clear out of my head.'

She ran from the hall in to the solar, returning almost immediately with what looked to Siward like a piece of folded cloth in her hands. Her eyes, he saw, had suddenly begun to shine. 'Send a messenger to Verduse tomorrow, with this.'

As she unfolded the black silk, he stared at the surcoat she had been making. On both sides she had embroidered a coat of arms such as he had never seen before. Then he realised it was exactly like the brooch Rollo had given her when he came back from Winchester one day. A tawny cat embroidered in gold thread with one up-raised paw. The long claws were open, clutching at a lightning bolt that had been split asunder, worked in fine silver thread.

'My lord's emblem and mine, forever joined. My servants here will retain their own colours with this emblem. If he agrees, the Guard will wear their own colours with this addition. Do you think he will like it? I have made a smaller one for Jarl's birthday. I want him to receive it without delay.' Alisandre hung expectantly on his answer.

'I shall despatch a man with it at first light, and he shall have the fastest horse we possess to speed him on his way.' He knew that each tiny thread had been sewn in love. She had stitched her heart into the work, for all to see. 'And I shall tell him to return here at the same speed with Lord Rollo's thanks.'

'I must be patient, I know, but how the time has dragged! I think it wise to write and tell him what has happened during his absence, do you not?'

Siward nodded, thinking to himself that she was also hoping the letter might bring Rollo back in all haste.

'You know, don't you?' Alisandre asked, her voice trembling slightly, and he looked at her in surprise.

'Know what, my lady?'

'I saw it in your face then. You have said nothing, but you must have heard . . .' She broke off, confused by the strange expression she had seen on his face for a brief instant as his thoughts took control. And embarrassed now, as she realised that perhaps he had not. Yet surely he was not deaf—and she had gone too far! 'The silly rumours about—about my lord Rollo—and another woman.'

'As you say, silly rumours. I dismissed them with the contempt they deserved,' came his unhesitating reply.

The next day, from a passing pedlar, Alisandre learned more of what was going on about the countryside as Prince John's Officers of the Crown, as they were known—who proved in many cases to be little more than greedy noblemen eager to line their own pockets with the hard-earned money of others—exacted from every Englishman one-quarter of all his goods and chattels. Many paid, for it was a royal decree and the money was sorely needed to return Richard to England. Precious wealth was handed over, accompanied by fervent prayers that the true king would soon sit on the throne again and that his upstart, ambitious brother would be banished to some far-off corner of the realm where he could do no harm. Others held back, protesting that they would be penniless in the years to come, unable to provide dowries for their daughters, education for their sons, and it was taken by force, often with an added levy for the trouble they had caused.

Roger Chabret and his men arrived at Wynterfold just before noon the following day. He was in a vicious, surly mood after the attack on them less than four miles from the boundaries of the estate in heavily wooded countryside. They had stood little chance against twice their number, and the four pack-mules, heavily laden with all manner of items from coin to plate, to casks of jewels, were led away under their very noses as they fought to defend themselves. Three men dead, six injured and one missing, either captured or deserted, hoping to gain a few coins for the information he could give the outlaws. Roger supposed they had been outlaws. There had been rumours of a band coming together in the Winchester area for some months, as Prince John's men roamed the country, taking excessive glee in their work.

Alisandre came down the steps from the keep to meet Chabret as he rode in, and he was irritated to see Siward at her side. So the Lord of Darkness had left a watchdog, after all!

'I have wounded men with me. They need attention, at once.' Chabret ignored Alisandre's companion and directed his words to her, his hands on his hips in an arrogant stance. 'And then, my lady, I will require your steward to show me your estate ledgers.'

Alisandre bristled at his rude manner. He had neither given her polite greetings nor acknowledged her position as mistress of Wynterfold. How glad she was of the efforts that had kept her up half the night! 'Your men will be well attended to, sir. And my steward, if required, is at your disposal. I have already drawn up an account that I shall be pleased to go over with you, when you have taken some wine with me. Siward, please see that Sir Roger's men have all they need, and then join us in the Great Hall.'

She had been expecting him, he realised, and he swallowed a goblet of cool red burgundy and held it out to be replenished. She seated herself at the table and indicated that he should do likewise. Her calmness irritated him, heightening the desire for revenge for the humiliation he had suffered over the loss of the pack-mules.

Siward came unnoticed into the Hall, and did not like what he saw. Roger Chabret was leaning over Alisandre's shoulder as she explained the account that she and Ponsford had made out for him. Aware at last of another presence, she looked up, and relief flooded across her features as Siward advanced towards the table. Chabret retreated, and once more took a seat across from her, again refilling his goblet. In silence she handed Chabret the list, and allowed him to peruse the final items for himself. 'I am to assume that you are to pay in coin what I could have taken in kind from the village. Is that right?' he demanded ungraciously, after a long while in which he flicked back and forth over the items.

'This tax, for all the worthy cause for which it has been levied, will bring great hardship to my people if you take the livestock which give them food and sustenance for the winter months. I think I have been fair in assessing the price of everything. Most of the total sum I have in silver coin, the remainder will be plate and some jewellery—my mother's—and of course I have not forgotten a contribution from my cousin. You may take what you wish from her rooms, I'm sure she would wish it for such a worthy cause.'

'Without Lady Margaret's permission?' Chabret raised a speculative eyebrow. What an entertaining thought!

'We all have to obey the prince's decree, my lord, do we not?' Alisandre returned sweetly. 'If you agree my figures, sir, I shall have the necessary money counted and at your disposal before nightfall. I am sure you have pressing business elsewhere.'

'I have wounded men,' he reminded her tersely. 'We shall be staying here overnight. I shall require a place for them to sleep, and, of course, a room for myself. This afternoon I shall look over the estate for myself. I am sure your figures are accurate, Lady Alisandre, but you have been such a short time here that there may be some things you have—shall we say— overlooked.'

For a moment her composure faltered at the thought of this man staying beneath her roof, even for one short night. 'If you must, my steward Ponsford will accompany you. Feel free to ask him anything you deem necessary.'

'I shall not require him,' Chabret returned, as he rose to his feet and pushed the papers she had given

him into his surcoat. 'I prefer to see things for myself.
I shall look forward to dining with you this evening,
my lady. We can discuss any irregularities—should
there be any—then.'

'The law of hospitality, which does not allow me
to turn you or your wounded men away when you are
in need of a place to sleep, does not also make it
necessary for me to endure your company a moment
longer than I have to,' Alisandre snapped, tight-
lipped, and a smile touched Chabret's mouth as he
watched a little more of the calm pose disintegrate.
'You are not welcome here, and I shall be obliged if
you will take your men and whatever else you have
come for away as soon as possible in the morning.'

'Your cousin, the Lady Margaret's, hospitality was
beyond reproach,' he said, and a flush crept into her
pale cheeks as she considered the extent of that
hospitality.

'I am fully aware of her generosity, sir...' She broke
off, biting back bitter words which had risen un-
bidden to her lips.

'Bar the door of your room tonight, my lady,'
Siward warned her with a frown as Chabret strode
from the room. 'He is not to be trusted.'

'His nearness makes me shudder, but I do not think
him foolish enough to risk facing you across a blade
again,' she answered.

She ordered a room to be prepared for the un-
welcome guest, and warned the kitchen-maids and
younger female servants to stay indoors, then quickly
went down to the solar to take up some more em-

broidery and occupy her mind with the delicate
stitching. Her gift of the tabard would bring Rollo
back quickly, she told herself, and concentrated more
fiercely on her sewing. She was brought rudely back
to life by the sound of someone cannoning into the
table beside her chair, and then a bitten-off expletive.
Her eyes flew open in alarm. She had fallen asleep!
Her needlework had slipped to the floor, and with
dismay she watched Roger's mailed foot step on it as
he came closer.

'So you decided to wait up for me after all, my
lady. You shall not be disappointed.' His words were
barely comprehensible, so slurred were they.

Alisandre shrank back in her chair as wine and ale
fumes were breathed full into her face. Chabret's eyes
were bloodshot, suggesting that he had been drinking
ever since he entered the house. Where was Siward?
How had the visitor managed to invade the solar
without being seen?

'You are intruding upon my privacy, sir. Please leave
at once,' she snapped, coming to her senses fully as
he reached out and cupped rough fingers about her
breast. 'Get out this instant!'

'Privacy, my lady? You only need that when you
are old and no longer attractive to men. For you, that
will be a long time. Don't play coy with me. I want
only what you have given others. Go ahead, scream,'
he mocked, as she opened her mouth.

The scream that rose in Alisandre's throat was
stifled by the fierce, nauseous pressure of his mouth
on hers. It was like being kissed by a wet haystack,

she thought in revulsion, as she brought up one knee, and in a very unladylike manner thrust it hard into his groin. Then her scream pierced the stillness of the room.

'Get up, you dog! Get up and look into my face before I kill you!' Siward's voice! Siward was directly behind him, the tip of his blade against the back of Chabret's neck.

'What shall I do with our friend Sir Roger? Loose this arrow? I hate to waste it on something so small and insignificant, so have you any other ideas on how he should meet his maker?' a voice drawled from across the room. Alisandre's startled gaze flew to the man who stood facing them, longbow drawn, an arrow pointing at Roger's back.

'My lady, perhaps you have some preference?' Will Appleton added, a smile touching his hard, thin face. 'I shall be honoured to despatch him in any way you see fit after all he has done this day, not only to you, but to innocent people who could not fight back.'

'I don't understand!'

'The men he took with him decided to amuse themselves with a few of the village women,' Siward told her. 'When they had finished, they set fire to some of the houses.'

'Dear God, have these men no scruples? No honour?' she cried, her own discomfort receding as she contemplated the orgy of rape and destruction they had perpetrated on her village. 'You and those brutes you call decent men will pay for this, Sir Roger Chabret, even if I have to go to Prince John himself.'

'My lady, you do not intend to allow him to leave here?' Siward asked in astonishment, coming to stand close beside her.

'If you harm him, we shall bring down the wrath of Prince John on our heads, and well you know it. I am not harmed, but he shall pay for what he has done to the village. It shall be deducted from what he takes with him. Enough for new homes for those who have none; food, clothing and livestock. I can do nothing about the men who attacked those poor unfortunate women. I wish to God Lord Rollo were here! He would not let them go unpunished. Now, find a safe place for Sir Roger. He is no longer a guest, so you can put him where you will. Preferably in chains, so that he gives us no more trouble tonight.'

'You high-handed bitch, you will pay for this!' Chabret snarled as he was hauled unceremoniously to his feet and thrust towards Will.

Siward's nose wrinkled in disgust as the odour of fear reached him. 'Somewhere near the sewage,' he said drily. 'He will be at home there.'

'You'll pay,' Chabret threatened. 'All of you.' In his drunken state, he had not yet seen any significance in Will's appearance.

'You can rest easy tonight, my lady,' Siward said. 'Everything will be taken care of. I shall place a guard outside your room until dawn, and another on the stairs. No one will pass them.'

'And in the morning we shall speed Sir Roger on his way,' she said without amusement.

CHAPTER NINE

WYNTERFOLD returned to its normal routine after the departure of Roger Chabret and his men, most bearing signs of battle that had not been upon them when they arrived, despite the previous attack. As Alisandre had surmised, Chabret was in no mood to argue when she thrust the papers under his nose with the altered tally, and he produced his own and allowed her to change these also. And then, in a mortified silence, his lips pressed tightly together, he signed the letter she had written. Only once did he hesitate when, reading it to the end, he discovered that not only had he assumed full blame for the actions of his men, the attempt to extort from Wynterfold more than its fair levy, but that he had, in a drunken moment, attempted to assault her. An act, she had written, unbecoming a knight and a man of honour. For a moment she had been quite disquieted to see that the indignant words caused him some amusement, but with the pricking of Siward's dagger against the nape of his neck, Chabret applied his seal.

'Let us hope I have not brought down the wrath of Prince John upon their heads and mine for what I have done,' Alisandre said with a faint smile. 'We must ride into Winchester tomorrow, Siward, I have

155

a long list of things to buy for my lord's home-coming, and Cook has given me an equally long one of spices and ingredients for Jarl's birthday. I think she believes I have invited a hundred guests!'

'I shall arrange an escort, my lady,' the man at her side returned respectfully.

On returning to Wynterfold her heart leapt unex-pectedly as they passed through the gates and she saw horses gathered before the steps. Rollo! But there was no sign of his big black horse, and the disap-pointment that engulfed her brought tears to her eyes. The figure dismounting with the help of a servant was instantly recognisable as that of her cousin Margaret. How dared she show her face here again, after what she had done! Alisandre fought against the anger that rose to consume her and banish all her well-meaning intentions. Then she noticed, dismounting after Margaret, the messenger she had sent to Verduse.

'Welcome back to Wynterfold. I regret I was not here to greet you.' The polite greeting brought a smile to her cousin's face as she began to ascend the stairs to the Great Hall. 'Will you not step in and take some wine with me? Have you had a long journey?' She restrained the urge to turn to the messenger, who was waiting at a respectful distance.

'I am exceedingly tired and shall go to my room directly. I shall talk with you later. We have much to discuss,' declared Margaret. She disappeared through the oak doors, leaving Alisandre staring after her with blazing eyes.

'Is there somewhere we can talk, my lady? Where we will not be overheard?' the messenger enquired, and she nodded and motioned him to follow her.

'Tell it to me from the beginning,' Alisandre ordered. She sat in Rollo's chair before the hearth, the goblet of wine beside her on the table untouched, despite Siward's insistence that she should take something for the shock she now received. It could not be true that Rollo was not at Verduse, and never had been there recently!

The man began his account. 'I made good time to France, my lady, and following the directions I had been given, I had no difficulty in finding the Château of Verduse. It was almost a ruin. Mostly blackened stones and charred beams, and there was a grave—no, I lie, two graves—quite close together behind the house. I spoke to an old man there who told me he was Lord Rollo's steward, and had been since his father's time. He had been left to care for the place, though, believe me, it needs little attention, and he has not seen Lord Rollo since December last year. I told him that Lord Rollo should have been there, and he said I was dreaming. He was most adamant that Lord Rollo would never again live at Verduse. He loathes the very sight of the place—and those are his exact words, my lady.'

Alisandre bit her lower lip, turning to Siward. 'Tell me, then, where is my loving husband? Do you know him better than I, who have borne his child, who love him still even though he has betrayed me beneath my own roof with another woman? Tell me where he is!'

Siward was silent. He had no answer, and dismissed the messenger.

Alisandre looked up towards the stairs. She rose to her feet slowly, like a sleepwalker, and turned away from him.

'Do you think it wise to approach Lady Margaret at this moment, my lady?' Siward began.

She wheeled on him, sudden fire in her eyes. 'I shall get to the bottom of this, and no one shall interfere. No one,' she repeated coldly.

'Come in, cousin. I was wondering when you would come to welcome me home.' Margaret turned her head as Alisandre came unannounced into the room. The maid brushing her hair was dismissed, and Margaret waved the other to a chair. 'Sit down and tell me what has been happening since I went away. It seems an eternity.'

'I do not think it long enough, cousin.' Alisandre's voice was without warmth, and the contempt in her eyes as she gazed at the woman reclining in a chair, barely covered by a loose robe, proclaimed that she was not the same trusting, emotional, little girl she had left behind. 'This is not your home any longer, and I shall be pleased if you will remove yourself as soon as possible. You are no longer welcome here. I shall not tire you with my reasons, for you are, I think, well aware of them. If this had happened to me four years ago...' She broke off as a smile spread across Margaret's face.

'What would you have done, my dear?' Margaret neither denied nor admitted the implication of the words. If Alisandre suspected the worst, so much the better. 'Had me whipped by one of your eunuchs? Boiled in oil?'

'You would not have smiled, cousin. Of that I can assure you.'

'You have gained new confidence, Alisandre,' Margaret purred. Outwardly she showed no signs of shock, but inwardly she was seething with rage.

Alisandre said resolutely, 'If you require any help with your removal, cousin, my servants will be pleased to assist you.'

To her horror, Margaret laughed and stretched languidly, like a cat flexing its muscles. The violet eyes gleamed with a malicious light. 'I am not leaving, my dear. I am home again where I belong. Wynterfold has been given into my charge. I have a paper, bearing your husband's seal, to the effect that until these rumours about you are either proved true—in which case, I think it will be *you* who depart for distant shores—or the falseness of them is established, I am to assume control here as mistress. Until Lord Rollo returns, of course.'

'I—I don't believe you. Show me! Rollo would never do this to me. Moreover, Wynterfold is not his to delegate to another. It is mine!' Alisandre almost choked over the words, her voice rising shrilly as the thin thread of her self-control drew nearer to snapping. 'Show me!' she demanded again.

'I have the paper safe, rest assured. When and if you make it necessary, I shall produce it. Alisandre, my dear cousin, think carefully before you go against me. It bears your husband's seal. I have only to show it to Prince John, as I shall if you prove troublesome, and I shall have fifty, nay, a hundred men here at my disposal. Your Guard will be useless.'

'What lies have you told your lover?' Alisandre demanded, stepping closer, her hands clenched into tight fists.

Margaret stared at her for a moment and then slowly rose from her chair as if not sure whether or not she might be attacked by this pale-faced goddess with blazing sapphire eyes.

'Lies? I think you are overwrought—and rightly so. I do understand how deeply you care for this place, my dear. After all, you manipulated Rollo so well in the Holy Land into obtaining it for you. He knew that the only way it would be yours would be if he killed my brother, and you made him want you so much that he obliged you.' Margaret's tone became suddenly hard, and jarred upon Alisandre's taut nerves like a axe being ground on a wheel.

Alisandre turned towards the door, refusing to allow herself to be drawn. 'You will give no orders in this house, cousin,' she declared icily,' and if you attempt to leave Wynterfold to go to Prince John and feed him more lies, I will have you stopped. Forcibly, if necessary. The Guard are and always will be loyal to me. Until Rollo returns, you will remain here.'

'As you wish, my dear. I am only carrying out his wishes, you know. I undertook the task because he asked me to do so. The part of chaperon does not really suit me,' she replied casually.

'My lord, shall we rest the horses awhile? We have been travelling for hours—since dawn,' Thomas Luckett said.

Rollo reluctantly brought his thoughts back to the present. Tomorrow they would reach Wynterfold. He had been thinking of Alisandre for the past hour, a half smile on his lips, which had deterred either of his companions from approaching him. They were travelling the long way home, avoiding main roads, and contact with villages and places that could have afforded them a decent night's rest and food. They were to reach Wynterfold without anyone knowing of their return, Rollo had told them when they set out from the coast.

'Ride ahead, Thomas. Find us a place to sleep in peace this night. If you can find nowhere that gives us protection from behind, then it will have to be in the open.'

Thomas inwardly groaned as he thought of yet another night shivering beneath the stars. He had not yet been with Rollo long enough to appreciate the wiseness of the decision.

They camped as it was growing dark beside a small stream, which gave them an opportunity to bathe some of the travel grime from their clothes and bodies. They ate a meal of cold meat, bread and cheese, washed down with the last of their wine, comforted by the thought that tomorrow would find them back at Wynterfold. Hot food, warm beds, safety.

Rollo thought he would send another message to Walter de Coutances to inform him of the success of his trips, and one to the Dowager Queen to reassure her that he had returned without mishap and would be continuing his dogged efforts to raise more money for Richard's ransom. There were many who had not yet given. Perhaps they needed a little persuasion, he mused, as he wrapped himself in his cloak and settled down to sleep. He would take Siward with him when he went collecting the next time. Perhaps it would make up for not being able to have him at his side for these past months, and it would end once and for all any rumours circulating about a breach between them. The Norseman was a loyal, trusted friend, and he would listen to no lies against him. He was feeling easier in his mind about everything, now he was almost home.

He tried to doze, a few feet away from Cerdic. Thomas stood watch amid the giant oak trees, for they had made camp in a clearing with no cover about them except heavy thicket and the dense trees. Ideal for an ambush, Rollo had thought, as he looked about him but acknowledged that all three were too tired to continue. Besides, no one knew of their return. Who was there to attack them so close to Wynterfold? This was Will Appleton's territory, and they had parted most amicably before Rollo departed for France. He yawned, and moved again to settle more comfortably on the hard ground. Tomorrow he would not have to dream of making love to Alisandre...

The ambush came without warning. Thomas barely had time to shout a warning before the men were upon them. A dozen of them, and well armed, Rollo saw, as he came to his feet, snatching up the sword that had lain at his side ready for the unexpected. He wheeled about, weapon coming up to meet the two men who leapt at him. One screamed in pain and fell back as the blade cleaved through his shoulder. His companion died less than a moment after, Rollo's axe buried in his chest.

'My lord—take care!' He barely heard Cerdic's cry, but he saw the look of horror that crossed the man's face as he started towards him—and at that instant felt a searing pain in his back. All was blackness.

'How long have I been unconscious? Where are we?' He opened his eyes on to two anxious faces bending over him. His right shoulder throbbed painfully. 'What happened? Did I faint?'

'No, lord, the coward that struck you hit you on the head, too, but he'll not stab another man from behind—I made sure of that,' Cerdic growled, adding quickly, as Rollo tried to sit up. 'Lie still a while longer. We are safe in this cave, I think.'

Rollo eased himself up on one elbow. The cave was just big enough to accommodate them all, provided they did not try to stand upright. Dare he risk lingering here? The blood suddenly drained from his face, and he slumped unconscious to the ground.

Thomas crossed himself as Cerdic thrust his hand inside Rollo's tunic. 'Is he . . .?'

'Lord Rollo—dead? Nay, it will take more than a knife to kill this man! Sleep, that's all he needs. The bleeding's stopped now. Let's cut some brush and be quick about it before they come back. Here, pile this across the entrance, and then cut another thick branch from that fir. I'll lead the horses away, and you follow. Make sure there are no tracks leading back to the cave.'

They were some way from the cave and about to return after tethering the horses to graze, when Cerdic lifted his head and sniffed the air. 'Smoke. I can smell smoke!' A red glow began to reach them through the trees, and for a moment both men stood stunned with shock. 'My God, they've found him! They've torched the brush . . . He'll be roasted alive in there!'

CHAPTER TEN

ALISANDRE was in the kitchen, supervising the preparations for Jarl's birthday, when she first heard the commotion going on upstairs. 'Find out what is happening,' she ordered one of the servants, as a cry rent the air. 'No! I shall go myself.' Patting a stray piece of hair back into place, she stepped towards the door and found it blocked by Siward's broad frame.

'My lady, I must speak with you.'

'What is it? What is all that noise?' Alisandre demanded. 'Siward, let me pass. I shall see for myself.'

'No.' She gasped as he caught her by the shoulders and pushed her back into the room. 'No, not yet. I must tell you ... God in heaven, how do I tell you?' he cried in an anguished tone. 'Give me a moment to find the right words.'

'To do what?' She was alarmed now. She had never seen him display so much emotion before. 'Rollo?' The name was a whisper on her lips. He nodded. She tried to free herself, but he held her fast, his face stricken with grief.

'There is no gentle way to tell you. Forgive me the pain I must cause. They were attacked on their way home. Cerdic and Thomas Luckett are wounded ... A sword-cut or two, nothing serious. But ...'

'No!' She clutched at him with nerveless fingers. 'He is not dead! He is hurt. That is what you are trying to tell me, isn't it? Badly hurt. Bring him in, let me tend him.' Alisandre almost screamed the words at him.

'There is nothing you can do, sweet lady. Nothing! He is dead!'

With sudden unexpected ferocity, she tore herself free and flung herself towards the door.

Barely one man looked at her as she advanced towards the cart where the body of a man lay draped with a heavy cloak. Cerdic stepped forward to block her way, and her voice shook with anger as she threatened, 'Get out of my way! By what right do you prevent me from looking on my husband's face?'

'Lady Alisandre, he is not the same...' Cerdic faltered.

Her fingers stole towards the covering, touched the stiff, lifeless hand which lay there and pushed it back. Was this her husband's hand? The skin was red and taut, as though it had been severely burned. A heavy gold ring adorned one of the mutilated fingers, and she caught her breath in horror. Rollo's crest. He always wore it on that little finger. She fought against rising nausea.

'He is not dead,' she stated firmly. 'Did Cerdic and Thomas see him in the flames? If so, where were they when he needed them? He cannot be dead... This man is not...' She pulled again at the cloth.

The scream which was torn from her lips echoed and re-echoed through her brain as she reeled back, anguish and revulsion now masking her distressed features. This—This mass of twisted flesh could not even belong to a human being, let alone to the fiercely handsome man she loved. The skin on the head had been drawn tight by intense heat until it was almost a skull. Little hair remained. What there was of it was black and singed. The deep-set eyes were thankfully closed. She wanted to look again, to force herself to search for the scars she knew so well, and which would tell her if this was truly he, but the courtyard was reeling around her, voices came to her as if from far off. She felt herself beginning to fall, and put out a hand for support. It touched that of the man on the cart—cold, chillingly cold—and again the sound of someone screaming echoed through her last moments of consciousness.

Rollo's body had been lifted from the cart and carried into the small chapel which adjoined the keep. There, it had been laid on a wide catafalque to await removal to his final resting-place alongside generations of de Greville-Wynters.

It was an hour before Alisandre had recovered sufficiently to drag herself from her bed and set her mind to the funeral rites she must perform for her husband, but her mind balked at seeing again that hideous countenance, touching those mutilated hands that had so often caressed her and brought her unique pleasure.

'Allow me the privilege of this last task, my lady?' Siward asked quietly. She had summoned him to help her to carry to the crypt the finest of Rollo's chainmail and halberk. The throwing-axe he had left behind, jewellery and precious possessions which would surround him during the long hours before the funeral took place on the morrow.

She nodded, choked with tears, and unable to speak.

The chapel was shrouded in shadow. The only light came from the four tall brass candlesticks that had been placed one at each corner of the catafalque. Beside one, in silent vigil over his dead lord, stood Cerdic, despite the throbbing wound in his leg. At a second, Guyon, who had openly wept as they carried Rollo inside. At a third stood Thomas Luckett, and by his own insistence—though he did not have the right, as a squire, to join the Guard in this—Gy, head downbent, his hands clasped tightly together in front. From time to time he raised his eyes slightly to look at the woman kneeling at the foot of the steps, but not once had she raised her head since she entered the chapel and assumed the attitude of prayer some four hours before. To one side of her, standing in the shadows, Siward watched the last of the villagers and servants from the house file past their dead lord, many crossing themselves as they turned away. Others, mainly the women, cast sympathetic glances at the grief-stricken woman who did not seem aware of their presence.

Alisandre had long since ceased to pray. Now she was lost in another world...Rollo's world of death and battles. The dimly-lighted chapel walls receded before her tired eyes, and in their place she beheld the walls of Acre, heard the victorious cries of the Crusaders as they followed Richard the Lion-Heart in the conquered city. And then quiet—the quiet of the garden below the Teacher's House where Rollo had taken her after he had carried her from the dungeons, believing her to be a captured Christian woman. No, he had never believed that! He had suspected her from the beginning, and made it known to her. Yet still they had been drawn together.

The night Tamir ibn Dak had foretold the future of the mighty Duke of Aquitaine, she had known they were destined to come together—that she would one day belong totally, willingly, to the Lord of Darkness!

'You were born under a dark star, my lord. Your name suits you well.' Such a frail old man, yet he had feared no man, not even Saladin himself. He respected greatness, honesty and truth, so what had he to fear?

'Tell me something I don't know. It has been dogging my footsteps since I left my mother's womb.'

'A woman will be your salvation. The right one, this time.' He had known even then—about Lisette and Verduse—about Karin, who would once again become Alisandre de Greville-Wynter and leave the land she had come to know. He had seen it in the stars. How she wished she could have his wisdom to guide her now!

'Your journey to Paradise has already begun, my lord. There is nothing you can do about it. Accept your fate.'

'*Insh'allah!* What is written is written. Then, for her sake, it would be better that we never meet!'

If she had not met him, she would never have known love. He had taken her to the highest peaks of passion, roused her as she was certain no other man could or would do. She would allow no other to touch her. She would remain true to Rollo for the short time she intended to remain on this earth. His dark star had touched her, too, overshadowing her life— bringing tragedy into it—but she regretted nothing.

'My lady, come away. You need to rest,' a voice whispered in her ear.

She did not move, ignoring Siward's entreaty. 'No!' She tried weakly to fend off the arms that held her, and cradled her against a mailed chest. 'I will not leave . . .'

As Siward swung round towards the door, her eyes fell upon the lifeless body of her husband, and the shuddering moan which broke from her made Cerdic clutch his sword more tightly and brought tears again to old Guyon's eyes. Her head fell back against Siward's shoulder, and the black veil slid away from her ashen cheeks and her eyes, now tightly closed. She was like one dead herself as he hurried with her away from the chapel, from the agony of her loss, the sympathetic eyes of servants and villagers—the disturbing gaze of Gy, who followed them to the door and stood watching as Siward ascended the stairs to the Great Hall with his unconscious burden.

*   *   *

The quiet dignity with which she conducted herself, and the composure she maintained despite the grief and agony she was surely suffering over her great loss, were admired and commented on time and time again by those who attended the funeral. Distant neighbours whom Alisandre had never met, yet whose acquaintance Rollo had made during his brief time at Wynterfold, arrived to pay their respects and to offer their condolences to the woman who received them with a gracious hospitality certainly not to be expected at such a time. They followed the procession of mourners, led by the widow herself, to the gently sloping hill behind the keep where generations of de Greville-Wynters had been laid to rest, and watched in silence as the plain, oak coffin was lowered into the ground.

Villagers who had stood back until those of importance had turned away to return to the house, now filed past the open grave, some dropping sprigs of thyme or evergreen on the coffin, an age-old custom to show the deceased person that he or she would not be forgotten.

Rollo's Guard lined up on each side of the grave and bent their heads in a moment of silent prayer before turning away to return down the slope.

Alisandre dropped sprigs of rosemary on the casket below, her lips moving in silent prayer. She looked down at the willow clutched tightly in her hand. The tree itself was a symbol of grief and lost love, and the leaves that fluttered down upon the rosemary contained her heart—her very soul. Forcing herself back, she turned slowly and went back to the house. As she began to mount the steps to the entrance to the Great Hall, she hesitated, and swayed slightly.

'My dear cousin, you look exhausted. Why don't you retire and allow me to see to your guests?' Margaret was at her side, clad in a velvet gown of dark mulberry trimmed with gold needlework.

Alisandre had been aware of her presence for some time, but had pointedly ignored her. Now she raised a dispassionate gaze to the face of the woman she had grown to despise. 'You are not mistress here yet, cousin! Need I remind you of that again?' she snapped, and her sharp tone brought three or four heads turning to see the cause of the dissension.

'But I shall be—soon—my dear. The sooner you accept that what is mine is shortly to be returned to me, the better for us all. Until then, I shall play the devoted relative, and none of these here today, whom you consider friends, will raise a hand to help you when I make my claim.'

In the sanctuary of her room, Alisandre discovered that she was trembling violently, and found it necessary to sit on a chair for several minutes. Her head began to pound. She leaned back against a cushion and closed her eyes, breathing slowly and deeply until the tremors passed. Then rising, she went to the door and turned the key in the lock, so that no one could disturb her.

Everything had been taken care of. The money-chests she had hidden from Roger Chabret were to be entrusted to Siward and used to keep them all. She knew they would be secreted from Wynterfold with the greatest caution, thus keeping them out of Prince John's greedy hands, or even those of Chabret himself.

With a sigh she began to undress, her mind suddenly at peace. There would be pain, but for a moment only, and then she would be with Rollo, never to be parted again. Clad in a loose robe over a sheer nightgown of pale blue silk threaded with silver embroidery—no idle choice this, for she had worn it on her wedding night in Jerusalem—she sat down before the mirror and began to brush her hair. When they met again, she would look as she had done that night and be received into his loving arms. Reality, the fear of death, began to drift away from her. Through death she would discover a new life with the man she loved. She could ask for no more.

She rubbed sweet-smelling musk into her skin, looking at herself this way and that like a woman who was indeed a bride, searching for some flaw that might not please the husband about to claim her. Her cheeks were pale, and she pinched them to bring some colour. The cloud of burnished gold fell about her bare shoulders in soft unbroken waves, framing her serene features, and her eyes that glowed with an almost feverish light in their blue depths.

From the bottom of Rollo's chest at the foot of the bed she took the basilard he had given her and slid it slowly from its leather sheath, a strange smile touching her lips as she remembered how she had

watched while he made it for her and his amusement
when she insisted on wearing it. Was he watching her
now, amused that she chose this very weapon with
which to take her life? Was he waiting as eagerly for
her—his longing to be reunited with her as great as
hers was for him? She would not accept that their
love could be bound by earthly chains. 'To those who
love as we do, nothing is denied us, Rollo my love,'
she whispered to the shadows about her. 'Your dark
star shall not part us. It shall have us both!' The blade
rose before her eyes, which widened as the candlelight
gleamed on the wickedness of the sharpened edge.
With a moan, she shut them tight and brought the
dagger down towards her heart . . .

'No!' Siward leapt from behind the curtain of the
antechamber where he had been hiding and his hands
closed over the weapon.

She heard him swear as the deadly edge cut into his
palm. She did not recognise the voice at that moment,
but was aware only that someone had stopped her—
taken from her the chance to be with Rollo again.
Strength flowed through her body like wildfire as she
fought him like a woman possessed, not daring to release her hold on the dagger, and it was only with a
supreme effort that he twisted it from her grasp. Not
knowing what she was about in the madness that was
upon her, Alisandre struck out at him, clawing at his
face with her long nails. With an oath, he flung her
back on to the bed. She came back up at him as he
sought to restrain her, eyes blazing, and in them now

was fear and anger and confusion, as she recognised him.

'Let me go! I command you.' She struggled against the hands that held her, her features working furiously. Her strength was ebbing...

Siward felt it and eased his grip. 'When you are calmer. Don't make me hurt you any more. Have you not suffered enough pain?' he pleaded.

'I shall have you whipped! Get out of my sight... I never want to see you again!' She screamed the words at him, and almost simultaneously there came a thunderous knocking at the door.

'If that is your wish, I shall do so, but only when you have promised me never to try this again.'

She blinked up at him stupidly. How dared he presume to tell her! And then she saw the blood on his face where she had clawed him, and realised that something warm and sticky was running over her hands and wrists.

'Siward...' Her voice was barely audible, as the realisation of what she had almost achieved flooded over her. She was still alive! Tears filled her eyes and began to course down her cheeks as the emotion she had so carefully held back now overwhelmed her, gave her blessed relief from the anguish tearing at her heart. Siward swore again as the door shuddered under heavy blows, and she could hear a multitude of voices. 'Send them away—please!' she entreated. 'I do not want them to see me like this. Tell—Tell them nothing.'

Siward had turned the key before realising the full impact of the scene which would be revealed to those outside, and then it was too late, for someone on the other side flung open the door, and a host of faces stared in utter disbelief at the dishevelled, tearful woman on the bed and then at the man who faced them, blood on his hands and face.

Margaret pushed her way to the fore, her lips twisting into a malicious smile as she regarded first Siward and then her cousin. 'So this is the way of it! Lord Rollo was right to think his wife was incapable of responsibility. No sooner is he in his grave than she entertains her lover in her room. The grieving widow no longer grieves! You will all bear witness to what we have seen here tonight. Remember it well. Look at her clothes! Is that a widow's attire?' She turned away, and slammed back into her own room.

Siward stepped towards the bed, hesitated, and then bent to retrieve the dagger from the floor. Alisandre's eyes widened, and she gave a cry as she saw that it, too, was covered in blood—his blood, not hers! 'Do not distress yourself further, my lady. I cannot bear it.'

'I could have . . . killed you!'

'Nay, the madness was on you for a moment only. It is nothing,' he assured her, snatching a linen kerchief from his tunic to bind his hand and stem the flow. The wound was deep beneath two of his fingers, and he found he could not move them. But she was alive, and at that moment nothing else was important to him.

'Oh, why did you stop me? How can you know what I suffer?'

'I know.' He gathered her in his arms, pressing her tear-streaked face against his chest.

It seemed an eternity before she grew quieter and lifted a trembling hand to wipe the last of the tears from her cheeks. Slowly she lifted her head and looked up into the face of the silent man who cradled her in his arms. She saw in his eyes such an expression of love that she felt her eyes grow moist again. Her fingers touched the scarred cheek that bore the ugly lines from her nails, and her lips quivered at the thought that she had inflicted pain on the one person whose concern for her far outweighed that of any other living soul.

'I would not have hurt you for the world. Not you!'

'It is past. Tonight must be blocked from your memory. What you tried to do—and also the way I am holding you now. It never happened. It will not again. Promise me!'

Mutely she nodded, but it was not enough. She felt his grip on her tighten, and forced the words through stiff lips. 'I promise.'

'Then I shall leave, easy in my mind.'

'I did not mean what I said, you know that! I was angry...confused. What would I do without you?' She was aghast to think her foolish words would drive him from her.

'Will you go to Shah'mat still, as you insist?'

'It was the only place I have been truly happy. Yes, I shall go there. There are papers over on the table. Take them, read them, give them...' Her voice trailed off as a great tiredness overcame her, and Siward felt her sink against him as if in a faint.

Gently he laid her back against the pillows, his face only inches from hers as her eyes closed. Carefully arranging the bedclothes over her, he turned towards the table, and froze in horror and anger at the sight of the figure who stood in the open doorway watching him.

'I've brought this for the Lady Alisandre,' Gy said. He held out a goblet wrapped in a napkin.

'Get out!' Siward shouted.

Gy turned and fled, spilling most of the posset before the door slammed noisily behind him.

Picking up the bundle of papers and parchments, Siward quietly left the room and went downstairs.

CHAPTER ELEVEN

ALISANDRE wandered in a frightening world of shadows and faces that were never very clear to her. Gigantic forms loomed before her vision and then receded without touching—without speaking. Rollo was lost to her for ever! She knew it now with a finality that weighed heavily on her heart. He had wanted her to join him, and she had fled from him in fear. She wanted to live, to bring up his son, and through him know again a different kind of love. Jarl, she was convinced, would be the image of his father, and each time she looked at him, each day she shared his company, it would be as though she were still with Rollo, for Rollo would live on in his offspring. Yet the terrible ache in her heart would never be dulled. For his sake, she must accept Siward's love as friendship only, and deeply wound him in doing so, but she could never think of him as anything but a friend. No desperation in her could ever drive her into the arms of another man, however worthy, and there was no nobler man on earth than he.

Oh, Rollo! Rollo, my love! In her restless dreams she uttered his name time and time again, her body unable to find comfort or rest in the huge bed. She wanted his hands upon her—his lips against her hair, her cheek, her breasts. She needed him! Oh, how she needed him!

In the heat of the June evening, she threw aside the covers and twisted and turned upon the feather mattress, her skin glistening with perspiration as another dream came upon her. She knew the room; it was the one in which she lay. Everything was the same: the table, and the stool before it; her table beneath the narrow window, where moonlight slanted across the silver-backed brush and comb. The room was dark with shadows, for the candle had burned down and had not been replaced.

Her mouth grew dry with fear as a shadow materialised from the darkness beyond her vision and slowly took on the shape of a man. No flowing cloak or horrible visage to send her screaming from the room, but a figure clad in normal garb, somewhat worn. She could see no face... It came closer, and she drew her hands over her body in abject terror. What was she to be presented with now? Had death appeared in yet another form to beckon her to Rollo's grave?

His face! The dark features grave and unsmiling as he bent low over her, his pale green eyes gleaming like iridescent pools beckoning her to their depths. His hands, touching her, wandering slowly, searchingly over her body, and she cried out and caught them to her, raising them to her cheeks. Warm flesh and blood, no ghastly apparition to tear her mind apart.

'Rollo! Rollo...' she whispered, lifting herself from the bed...

She was seized in a fierce grip, and the lips that clamped over hers, forcing them apart with brutal passion, silenced her. She responded with an eagerness born of desperation, a low moan of pleasure rising in her throat as her nightgown was pushed aside and hot kisses trailed across her naked skin. His caresses seared her skin, sending tongues of fire along her thighs, her stomach. This was a dream she did not want to end...

Something was wrong! At first she could not define what, and then, as memory returned and with it a reality she did not want but was forced to accept, she began to push at the hands which explored between her thighs, parting them for the final assault.

Her soft skin had been scored by something rough—a beard! Rollo wore no beard, and was meticulous about being clean shaven. This man was not her husband! She cried out, struggling against the arms confining her against a sinewy body hard with muscle. Dear God, who was trying to violate her? She struck out, screaming simultaneously, but her hands met only empty air.

'It was no dream,' Alisandre repeated for the tenth time at least. 'There *was* someone in my room.'

Siward was alarmed by the feverish light burning in Alisandre's eyes. She beckoned him to the bed, caught at his hand and drew him down beside her. 'What have you found? Tell me!' she begged.

'I am sorry. Nothing. No one.'

She became aware that she was clutching his hand. She frowned at the bandages beneath her fingers, and then raised shocked eyes to his face. 'Your hand! Dear heaven, I remember now. The dagger! Oh, Siward, I had forgotten.'

'The wound is almost healed,' he told her, gently withdrawing it from her grasp. It was true that the gashes had mended, but he had two dead fingers, the nerve-ends severed by the blade. In combat, his sword-arm would be useless.

'Do you think I am losing my mind?' She lay back amid the pillows. 'Be truthful. The terrible thing I tried to do, and now... tonight... I swear by all that is holy that there was someone in this room, and for a moment he did look like Rollo. I know it could have been my imagination, but I did not imagine a man's hands on me...' She closed her eyes, remembering how she had welcomed the touch, the kisses, the fire which swept through her body. 'Only *he* could ever make me feel like that!'

'As soon as you are well, you are summoned to the court of Prince John,' Siward told her with great reluctance. 'The Lady Margaret left here two days ago, and the messenger came this morning. We can only guess what she has been saying.'

'That I entertained a man in my bedchamber, with my husband not cold in his grave! She has gone to give Prince John the paper Rollo signed. I cannot stay in this bed. I must fight her!' Alisandre started up, but her senses reeled at the sudden movement and the blood drained from her face. With a soft cry she fell back, tears starting to her eyes. 'I am so weak!'

'Something else has happened,' Siward said quietly. 'It is best that you know all now. Two days ago a horse came up to the main gates. Across his back was a dead man. There was a note attached to his clothes that said simply, "A present for the Lady Margaret from Will Appleton". Cerdic recognised him as one of the men who attacked them. He was also one of your cousin's retainers. Within the hour, she had left the house. Ask yourself now, my lady, who was really behind the attack?'

'Why should Margaret want Rollo dead? They were lovers!' The words were out before she could contain them. 'It's true, she told me so herself. Not only did she spent a night with him here, but also at the coast. We know he never went to France, so he must have been with her.'

'We do not know that for certain,' Siward broke in, hating to see the pain in her eyes as she spoke. 'There are too many unanswered questions. Do not judge yet. Do not forget that Lord Rollo was to deliver money to the Dowager Queen for King Richard's ransom.'

'It is of no importance now. Neither of us has him.' Alisandre replied. 'Bring me something to make me strong and well quickly. I shall need all my wits about me when I face cousin Margaret and her royal lover!'

Alisandre slowly rose, and waited patiently for Prince John to acknowledge her.

He was not quick to do so. His stony gaze carefully scrutinised her appearance, but he was unable to find fault with the woman who stood before him in the garb of a widow, pale faced, but proudly defiant. 'Lady Alisandre, I wish I could greet you under more—shall we say—desirable circumstances.'

Alisandre approached nearer to the dais where Prince John sat, her head held high. She looked neither to the right nor the left. Her gaze was centred on the richly-clad figure of Richard's brother, and the woman who took an important place at his side. Her steps faltered as Margaret bent her head and whispered something to the prince. She was alone, she realised, as she swept down in a low curtsy, hating herself for acknowledging this man who sought to steal his brother's throne, but knowing, for her own sake and that of those she considered friends, that she must show him his due as a prince of the realm. No matter what took place here today, she would not forget the mysterious circumstances under which Rollo had met his death. If she did not find retribution here—and justice—she would seek it elsewhere, without thought of the cost.

'May I ask why I have been summoned here, Sire? If it is to answer the question of who shall have control of Wynterfold, there is no question. The estates are mine by right of inheritance.'

There were gasps from several onlookers. Murmurs of approval, even of admiration, from others. The natural scowls of John's cronies. She had taken the initiative without hesitation, knowing that boldness was her only chance—her only defence against whatever was in store for her—to attack first.

The irritation that sprang into Prince John's face told her how unwise and dangerous her boldness was, but she stood her ground, her gaze never wavering from his face.

'In such matters, I shall have the last word, madam. I suggest you remember that.'

'Believe me, it is stamped on my mind, Sire,' Alisandre returned.

She was openly challenging him, he realised, and his anger increased. Then he leaned back in his chair, a smile touching the corners of his thin mouth. 'Good, we understand each other, then, so we can proceed with the matter in hand. I have been handed a letter, bearing the seal of the Duke of Aquitaine, to the effect he wishes the Lady Margaret de Greville-Wynter, your cousin, to assume control once more of the estate we know as Wynterfold. You have some comment on this? I find it a strange document. Why should he do such a thing?'

'I have seen no document,' Alisandre said coldly. 'If one exists, it is a forgery.'

'I said I have seen it, my lady. Are you questioning my word?'

'No—No, of course not. But I can only assume that my husband was tricked into writing it. As you say, Sire, why should he? We have been at Wynterfold for a short while only, but while there he was content—and there are many witnesses to this—to leave the running of the house and the estate to me. He presided over matters concerning village quarrels, ownership disputes and the like, but otherwise he did not interfere.'

'Until perhaps he began to suspect that your interest was not totally involved with Wynterfold alone?' John suggested with narrowed gaze, and she barely suppressed the gasp which rose to her lips. What was he suggesting?

'I do not understand you, Sire.' She felt as if a net was tightening about her, and Margaret's confident smile as she flicked a speck of dust from her silk sleeve did nothing to ease her growing apprehension.

'Your husband spoke to me of his reluctance to leave you alone—well, almost alone—during his absence,' Margaret murmured with a soft laugh. 'He feared temptation might prove too strong for you.'

'As it did for you, cousin,' Alisandre answered sweetly. 'How dare you judge my morals, when your own are lower than those of a camp-follower!'

'While the Lady Alisandre's past is somewhat questionable, we are not here today to discuss that aspect of her life, but to consider the request—nay, the demand—of the Lady Margaret, and in this I order, having read the document she has given to me, that Wynterfold be returned to her.'

Alisandre's heart sank as Prince John waved a man forward from behind his chair. Her eyes fastened on the scroll he carried, and the breath caught in her throat as it was unrolled and presented to her. Rollo's handwriting—such a bold scrawl, like the man himself! His seal! Siward had been right. 'As far as

I can see, it is my husband's seal.' Her admission was delivered in a clear, unwavering tone, betraying none of the hopelessness inside her. 'But I accuse the Lady Margaret de Greville-Wynter, my cousin, of being involved in the death of my husband. I know not how. I only know she hated him, as she does me. She holds us responsible for the death of her brother.'

'Your accusation is ludicrous, Lady Alisandre, and completely without foundation,' John snapped. 'I will accept that you are overwrought at the death of your husband. We will speak of it no more. As to the question of the estates...' He felt Margaret's fingers again caress the back of his hand, and sensed her puzzlement when he withdrew it, ignoring the gesture. 'I have several possible solutions to the question. One is to leave things as they are and declare the document you have seen to be a forgery, but—as you have stated—it is not. Therefore, in all fairness to the wishes of your late husband, I should return Wynterfold to your cousin. However...' He paused, to allow the full attention of everyone to focus on his words. They would cause a stir, he knew, and he cast a sidelong glance at the woman beside him as he continued, 'There is one option that will have my deepest consideration. If Wynterfold were in the hands of a man, I should have no objection to over-ruling the petition that has been presented.'

Alisandre felt only confusion at the Prince's words. What man?

'Once the mourning period for your husband has lasted for six months—an eternity for one so young to be alone—I shall expect you to take another husband.' He paused again, and met Margaret's daggered gaze without a qualm. 'Sir Roger Chabret has already asked for your hand. In those circumstances, your estates would be in capable hands, controlled by a man with considerable experience in such matters, and I would be content.'

'I shall never marry again. Never!' Alisandre sprang to her feet, trembling from head to toe at the outrageous suggestion. 'Marry that—that lecher who sought to rape me beneath my own roof! I have a confession, signed in his own hand!'

'I do not think we should go into that too closely,' John snapped. 'Chabret's version of the incident does not tally with yours, my lady, and he has witnesses.'

'To lie for him!'

'I have decided! Your arrogance has forced the issue. Within the year, you will wed Sir Roger. If you do not, you will forfeit the estates to the Lady Margaret.'

Alisandre stood speechless before the prince, her face drained of all colour, then she stepped back.

'I shall never marry again! I ask all here today to bear witness to my words. I shall not be coerced, and if my premature death should solve the problem, I pray there will be those who will question what has happened here today. I have never betrayed my husband. When you have had such a man as I have, no other is necessary, even after death! I shall fight for my rightful inheritance. It was my father's, and his father's before him, granted by a king of

England.' She saw John stiffen with anger at the taunt, but she was beyond caution. 'With your leave, Sire, I shall withdraw and return to Wynterfold. My cousin is not welcome there, and will be refused entry should she arrive. If you send men against me, I will fight as my husband would have done before me. You may consider me to be of dubious background but I know I have the blood of a proud Saxon warrior in my veins and I know he would never have submitted to the blackmail you propose. Your leave, Sire!' She swept down into a deep curtsy, her eyes veiled.

For a long moment John's eyes considered her and the challenge she had thrown down. 'You have my permission to retire, Lady Alisandre. Think well on my words. You will, of course, not object to Sir Roger visiting you from time to time and paying his respects. Perhaps, in time, you may find him quite . . . acceptable.'

CHAPTER TWELVE

'WHAT ARE we going to do?' Siward asked, looking at Alisandre with a frown. She had barely spoken to him since they left Winchester, and he had been loath to interrupt her thoughts, but now they were almost home, and he was growing concerned. 'Will you refuse the Lady Margaret entrance to Wynterfold, despite John's command? We shall need more men.'

'We?' Alisandre lifted her head and gazed into the scarred face, a softness in her eyes that reached out and touched his heart. 'Have I not asked enough from you, my friend? You must not involve yourself in this. My quest for revenge may lead me to my death.'

'Not while I have breath in my body!' Siward vowed. His hand closed over the bridle of her horse, easing it to a halt. 'You can be gone from England before they realise it. Let your cousin have Wynterfold—and Chabret. They are made for each other! Before a week is out, I swear one or both will be dead. She will never forgive him his treachery—or for wanting you, I suspect!'

A faint blush of colour rose in her cheeks as she considered being wife to Roger Chabret. 'Nor will he forgive you for that night,' she returned with a shake of her head. 'No, I cannot leave, but Jarl must. I want you to escort him and the others to Shah'mat. I know they will be safe with you.'

'And you?'

'I am convinced that Margaret was somehow behind Rollo's death. And she had the help of Chabret. If I must—accept—their presence at Wynterfold in order to discover the truth, I will.'

'Will you also tolerate his hands on you, while she watches and gloats that the revenge she seeks for her brother's death is almost satisfied?' Siward demanded, his voice harsh with emotion.

'So you have realised it, too. I will never marry him—or submit to him,' Alisandre said. 'But if I appear to accept Prince John's command that I do, who knows? I might be able to play on Chabret's hatred for Margaret and his desire for me.'

'You tread a dangerous path. He is not a man to be patient.'

'I know. I have to do this, Siward—for Rollo. Do you understand?'

'That you will always love him? That not even your son's life was important to you when you had lost him?' Siward's tone was etched with bitterness, his features bleak, as he nodded. 'I understand, and I accept all this. In return, you must accept that I shall always love you. I feel for you as you do for him. Will you deny me what you demand for yourself? I shall not leave you. If this is what you want to do, I shall stand beside you and help you in any way I can.'

'You risk Chabret's anger,' she warned, yet she could not deny him what he asked. How she needed someone she could talk to and confide in. He would never betray her trust.

'If he calls me out, I shall kill him. A simple solution to your problem,' he retorted with a shrug.

'And find yourself in one of John's dungeons! No, that is not the way—at least not until I have the proof I need. Then you may do as you wish with him before we depart. I pray we shall live to reach Shah'mat again.'

'My lady's attentions to another man may well provoke my ire!' Alisandre looked at him sharply, only to find him smiling. 'I may be tempted to seek consolation elsewhere,' he added meaningfully. 'Attack from all sides, no?'

'Margaret? No, Siward, she is too cunning an opponent. She would never believe . . .' She was stunned by the lengths he would consider to help her.

'She has offered me her bed on more than one occasion. Perhaps I should accept?'

'She destroys everything and everyone she touches! I wish you would reconsider . . .'

'We have but one aim—to seek out the truth and deal with those responsible for Lord Rollo's murder. Is that not so? How it comes about is not important, if we succeed.'

'Siward!' The startled cry was wrung from Alisandre's lips at the sight of the men who had stolen silently out from the heavy foliage to surround them completely. Longbows drawn, arrows pointing at Siward's heart, they stood without speaking.

Siward's mouth tightened into a grim line as he scanned the bushes, and then the faces of the outlaws menacing them. His gaze became fixed on the tall, thin man who came into view, pushing his way through the outlaws. Appleton!

'My lady, tell your man not to touch his weapon. I want no bloodshed here today. My orders are to capture you unharmed.'

'Capture?' Alisandre echoed, her throat growing dry with fear. 'By whose command do you apprehend us?' she demanded.

'No questions now, my lady. Please allow one of my men to lead your horse. I shall have to use force, if you make it necessary,' Will Appleton said, as her eyes began to blaze. 'You are in no danger, either of you, at least, not from my men or from me. I cannot answer for... Come.' He turned away, indicating that they should follow.

She cast a desperate glance at Siward, not knowing what to do.

They had not gone far when Will Appleton held up a hand, and his men halted. He came back to stand beside Alisandre's horse, and said in a quiet but firm tone, which told her he would resort to the force he had mentioned if she refused, 'I must bind your eyes, my lady. We are hunted men, and we do not want Prince John's soldiers down on us.' He motioned to the silk scarf at her waist, and slowly she untied it and held it out to him, but he indicated that Siward should tie it about her eyes.

When he made no move, his face tight with anger, she said urgently, 'Do it! There is nothing else for it.'

'Not now,' he growled, as he bound the silk about her eyes.

For an instant she felt his hand cover hers, re-assuring in its strength. The reins were taken from her grasp, so that she was totally in darkness and at the mercy of the man who guided her horse. A tremor of fear ran through her, but she overcame it.

'Guard your emotions, my friend,' Will warned, as he stepped back. 'Or you will not live to see the sun set this day. I have no quarrel with you—or with her. Your foolishness is your own, but I cannot answer for others...'

'Who?' Siward cried hoarsely, as he submitted in an agony of tumult to having his own eyes covered. 'To whom do you deliver us?'

'There is one to whom she must answer—and you. Against him, I do not think either of you will have any defence,' came the chilling answer.

Alisandre gripped the pommel of her saddle tightly as the words reached her, her mind racked with questions. A low branch caught against her hair, and she cried out as it whipped free suddenly and cut across her face. When she touched her cheek, she felt blood upon her fingers. Now, she was truly afraid!

It seemed hours before her horse was brought to a halt. She heard voices close by, and reaching up, she tore the scarf from her eyes. They were in a large clearing, and surrounded by armed bowmen, sullen-faced, suspicious-eyed men who looked at her as if she were an enemy!

Siward dismounted, and lifted her to the ground. The frustration she sensed mounting in him alarmed her. 'Do nothing,' she begged. 'Let us find out why we are here, and make some bargain with him for our freedom.'

'I no longer trust him...' A fierce expletive broke from his lips.

She followed his gaze, and beside the fire where several men squatted watching a deer being roasted on a crude spit stood two men in familiar garb. 'Traitors!' Before Siward could stop her, she strode across to them, and her riding-whip cut deeply across Thomas Luckett's shoulders and chest. As he reeled back, throwing up an arm to protect himself—while in no way trying to disarm her—she wheeled on Cerdic, her eyes blazing, her face ashen, despite the heat of her anger. 'You have betrayed me! Why? Who has paid you? Carrion! If I were a man, I would see you die slowly and in great agony for this. By whose authority do you surrender me into the hands of outlaws?' She was beside herself with rage at this final act of betrayal.

A man rose from beside the fire—tall, dark of features, with pale green eyes that glittered as his hand caught the upraised whip and stayed another blow. In the depths of them she saw such fury, such condemnation, that she felt as though she were looking into the fires of hell. She tried to speak, but no words would pass her lips. Her disbelieving gaze swept down from the bleak features to the hand that held her wrist. He wore no ring—yet she needed no proof to tell her who this man was... He who had stood at the foot of her bed as she lay delirious; he who had sat at her side, held her in his arms, he whose lips had covered hers, whose hands had once again roused her when she thought herself devoid of all life, all feeling.

'By my authority, Kutti,' Rollo, Duke of Aquitaine, said coldly. 'They do but obey my commands, as always. I still have some loyal men to do my bidding,' came the additional taunt, and his deep voice was laced with sarcasm and something more that made her heart grow cold. Rollo, alive? Yet had she not always known it in her heart—or had it been in her dreams?

'Rollo!' She sank against him, the whip falling from her grasp. She clutched at his rough homespun shirt, heedless of the pain in her cheek where the branch had cut her. Joy spread through her like wildfire. Rollo alive! Tears flowed over her cheeks and fell upon the hand she clutched. Instantly she felt him tense, and she looked up in puzzlement. 'Why do you look at me so—so—strangely?'

'Tears will not sway me,' came the terse retort.

'Sway you from what?' she cried. Was this another nightmare from which she would awake to find herself in bed, soaked with perspiration, losing him again to the dark shadows of night? No, he was flesh and blood—alive! He had deliberately sent Cerdic and Thomas Luckett back to her with another man in his place. She had buried a stranger—and he had planned that she should! How could he have deceived her, and brought her such pain! 'Of what am I accused, my lord?'

'Of adultery, madam. And you are here so that I shall deliver judgement on you.'

'Judgement—on me?' Alisandre gave a shrill laugh and stepped back from him, anger beginning to burn in the depth of her eyes. 'Surely I should stand in judgement on you, for your betrayal of me with my own cousin! For the lie you perpetrated in allowing me to believe you were dead! For the anguish you have caused not only to me, but to your son! We are obviously of no importance in your eyes now that you have a new interest. I was a fool to think you would ever give your heart to one woman... You do not have one to give!'

The flat of Rollo's gloved hand caught her a stunning blow across one cheek and sent her reeling into Siward's arms. Rollo's mouth twisted into a sneer as he saw the way the Guard's arms closed so readily round her and she made no effort to pull herself free. She condemned herself!

'You are wrong, my lord Rollo.' It was Siward who gently eased her away from him. 'I know not who has fed you these lies, although I have my suspicions that they were whispered across a pillow.'

The taunt struck home, and Rollo's eyes narrowed to green slits as he regarded this man whom he had once been stupid enough to consider a friend. 'Curb your tongue if you wish to see another sunrise!' he snapped.

Siward stood his ground, unperturbed by the rage he could feel emanating from his lord. He folded his arms over his chest, facing him as an equal, and the stance made Rollo's brows draw together into a fierce frown.

'Many years ago I fought a man just like you,' he said heavily. 'A man I had called friend. A man I trusted with my wife...as I trusted you with—her!' He glared at Alisandre, and it took all her courage not to recoil from the enmity in that swift glance.

'She is innocent of the things you accuse her of,' Siward retorted. 'Show me the lying cur who dares cast such a slur on her good name! Let him say the same words to me, and I will choke them from his lying throat. And then, my lord, I will take from you what you no longer want. I told you I would do so if the day ever came when you abandoned her. I believe it now has!'

'No!' Alisandre pushed her way between them, striking aside the hand that Siward stretched out to restrain her. 'How dare you barter for me as if I were some—some chattel to be sold to the highest bidder on the block! No one shall fight for me. I forbid it. Let he who accuses me of adultery step forward and face my wrath. He will answer to me, and to no one else.'

'As you will to me, Kutti,' Rollo told her. His gaze swept down to the hem of the beautiful black gown that trailed in the dirt about her feet, and then slowly wandered upwards, insulting in its intense scrutiny. The green pools darkened as they came to rest upon the crowning glory of her hair, and she saw a contemptuous smile deepen the corners of his lean mouth. 'I see you have not shorn yourself. So much for your protestations of undying love. Like all women, you are an expert liar.'

Unconsciously Alisandre lifted a trembling hand to touch the plait. In her grief, she had forgotten the words she had spoken to him that day in their bedchamber as he loosened her hair before they made love. Colour flamed into her cheeks. How could he believe that because she had not carried out that promise, she no longer loved him! How could he be so blind!

'"I belong to you and no other"', Rollo reminded her grimly. 'You lied then, as you will lie now when you try to make me accept you have not been unfaithful. Take care, Kutti. Your very life hangs in the balance—not just that head of beautiful hair!'

'I am not afraid of your threats, Rollo.' Her head tilted back proudly as she looked up into the bearded face. 'I have been used by you in the most despicable fashion possible. Your reasons are beyond me, but I shall never forgive you—no matter if my life-span be another twenty years or less than another day. I laid another man in a grave, and wept over him because I believed him to be you. I...' She swallowed the words that sprang to her lips. She would never tell him how she had attempted to take her life. In his present frame of mind, he would never admit that she was capable of such an act of self-sacrifice. 'Your son is without a father—a father whom I thought loved him, cherished him, as I thought, in my misguided way, that he cherished me, that we would be together always. I have been abandoned for months on end, almost raped by a drunken brute. I have been accused of adultery and worse before Prince John's grinning apes at court, and commanded to marry again before the year is out! For love of you, I was going to fight. I wanted to avenge your death!' Her shrill laughter bordered on hysteria, and instinctively Siward moved a pace closer, his gaze challenging his lord to stop him.

Rollo said nothing. He could not drag his eyes from the flushed face of the woman confronting him ... It was as if he had suddenly been struck dumb. Her words seared his brain, yet he fought against accepting them. To do so would be to accept that she was innocent, and he had proof that she was not. Like Lisette, her need for consolation had outweighed that of her wifely duties. Why had he ever thought her different? Yet she was. There would never be another woman with her fire, her childlike innocence. Damn her! Innocence—she and Siward? He had been in love, and he had been blind. Never again would that happen, especially not now, when he needed all his wits and all his senses to hold back from the allure reaching out to him, the memories which came crowding in on him, threatening to weaken his resolve. She had betrayed him! She must pay!

'You—stand in condemnation of me?' Alisandre cried, no longer able to contain a tumult of emotions. 'You? Whom were you looking for that night when you came to my room, Rollo? Whom did you think you were kissing? Whose body were your hands caressing? Did you mistake me for Margaret, perhaps?'

'You are from the same mould! You shall have a chance to answer your accusers, madam. Prepare yourself!'

'Prepare myself! Like a lamb to the slaughter! What has happened to him?' Alisandre whispered miserably. They had been escorted to a bare, wattle hut and left alone, but a guard had been set to watch them and prevent their leaving. From a small window opening she had observed her husband deep in conversation with Will Appleton and Cerdic, and the anger in her had multiplied. 'Has the accident turned his mind? I know what grief at the loss of him did to me, so is it possible that his suspicions could also wreak havoc on his mind?'

'His jealousy has got the better of him,' Siward replied grimly, 'as I one day feared it might. He loves you too much.'

'Love!' She wheeled away from the window to face him with a derisive look. 'Possession of something he desires, subjugation to his will, yes, but love? No, he does not love me. I begin to doubt that he ever did. When I think of how it was between us, I cannot believe... Yet I must! If he had loved me, he would not have made me believe him to be dead, for he would have known what it would do to me. Have I not told him time and time again that I have no life without him? Yet he did so—he took from me my world—

and now *he* stands in judgement of *me*! For what crime? For remaining your friend and refusing to allow the lies of others to ruin what we share? In its way, it is as precious to me as my love—the love I once had for Rollo.'

'Never say that to his face, I beg you!' Siward was concerned by her show of spirit.

'He is not the man I knew and loved,' Alisandre said in a low tone.

'Do you not love him still?'

'Yes—God help me!' Her tone was muffled, choked with tears. 'I do. If he had reached out and touched me, taken me in his arms, shown me one brief moment of compassion, of understanding, I would have forgiven him everything.' She gave a bitter laugh. 'But that's what he wanted me to do. What he was waiting for. Me—to throw myself on his great mercy! No doubt he would have generously forgiven me my—indiscretions! What has happened to him? How could he taunt me so cruelly with the things we have shared?' Her hand strayed to her hair, and almost absently her fingers began to pluck out the pins retaining the plait. Still not looking at what she was doing, she began to unbraid it, ran her fingers through the red-gold cloud that descended about her shoulders and fell past her waist. She could not remember the last time she had cut it. 'Give me your knife, Siward,' she commanded.

'No, you shall not touch it. I will not let you!'

'It must be done. My husband is dead. I do not know this man. He has Rollo's eyes, Rollo's face, his voice, but he is a stranger to me.'

'Then fight him! For your own sake, fight, or he will destroy you!' he urged. Dear heaven, he felt so useless!

'I cannot fight him, Siward. I love him too much, no matter what he has done to me.'

'Then you force me to do it for you, and I shall. You will not stop me,' he vowed, shutting his mind to the useless hand that would be his death-warrant. Barely able to hold a sword, he stood no chance against Rollo, but she did not know that, and he would give a good account of himself. Perhaps the gods would be on his side, for a change!

'You have sacrificed enough for me.'

'Someone has to protect you against yourself.'

No one came near them for over an hour, then a man appeared in the doorway and beckoned them to follow him. Alisandre paused for a moment, gathering all her courage, then, picking up her skirts, swept proudly out of the hut towards the fire.

Siward followed a step or two behind. He searched the sea of faces around the fire and found the boy there, standing close behind Rollo, his young face bearing a satisfied smile as Alisandre came to a halt in front of her husband. Gyl! So much the boy must have seen and misinterpreted, and Rollo, his mind embittered by past treacheries, accepting his word as truth, had condemned without a hearing the woman he loved. That was why they were here now. To be judged on the word of a foolish boy who had never known the agonies of love, and sought only to find favour in the eyes of his master.

'Be seated, Kutti. You must be hungry.' Rollo motioned her to a place beside him. She lowered herself cautiously on to the hard bark, not trusting the half smile on his lips as his eyes considered the long hair about her shoulders, nor the lack of venom in his tone. 'Bring wine and food for my lady. Let us show her that hospitality exists even among wolves.'

Alisandre flushed at his use of the word. Did he consider himself one of this band of outlaws? Was this how he preferred to live? 'I have no appetite,' she lied, refusing the wooden platter of venison thrust out towards her. She also declined the horn of wine. 'You live well, my lord,' she remarked, after watching him consume the contents of his platter and then wash it down with a cool draught. 'You fill your stomachs on the king's deer. Do you also fill your pockets on the money intended for his ransom?'

'Take care, Kutti! My loyalty has always been with Richard, and well you know it. I do not steal from him—ever. I take only from those who would deprive him of his throne. From John, not from Richard.'

'Know, my lord? What do I know? You left me alone at Wynterfold while you returned to France, to Verduse, which you were to restore to its former grandeur so that we—your son and I—could live there, did you not? No, you did not!' Her voice rose, as he turned and looked at her with green eyes flashing a warning. 'Pray do not be reticent in speaking out. Let he who would condemn me also prepare to be condemned. You left me alone with a lie! You never went to Verduse. You never intended to. You—and my cousin—were together at the coast, where you remained. Siward wanted me to believe that you were a courier for the Dowager Queen, but I cannot accept that. If you were—if you were as loyal to Richard as you pretend—if you were about her bidding, you would not be skulking here with—with these men. You would never have allowed people to believe you were dead. The Lord of Darkness I knew would never hide behind others!'

'If I had not, Kutti, if I had not perpetrated this charade, I would indeed be dead—at the hands of your dear cousin! They were not her men, but I swear the order came from her to lay the trap which almost killed me,' Rollo flung back bitingly. 'Ay, we met on the coast, a day after I had returned from France. As you say, I never intended to go to Verduse, but I was sworn to secrecy and could tell no one—not even you.'

She had been right! Margaret *was* behind it all. Still, even though she accepted that he was telling the truth, she found herself demanding, 'Why should she wish you harm? She was your mistress and, from all accounts, deep in your favour. Why else would you have given her that—that insulting letter? To deprive me of Wynterfold! To give it to her as if I—I were nothing, a mere child! You had no right . . .'

'I gave her nothing.' Rollo's voice cut across hers angrily. 'It was a forgery!'

'I saw it with my own eyes. Prince John showed it to me. It was your hand—your seal,' she flung back bitterly.

'Your eyes deceived you, woman!' he thundered, and a few men moved uneasily in their places.

'Perhaps she stole it from you while you slept?' Alisandre mocked. 'It would be so easy to believe that once—but not now. You have betrayed me with her too many times. With who knows how many others.'

'You—You dare to say that to me!' She flinched at the fury blazing out of his face, but knew that to show her fear would be the worst thing she could do. 'You, whose name stinks of infamy? I had not been away a few weeks before you were provoking gossip.'

'There are always those who will blacken the name of a woman alone,' she retorted. The light was fading, and as someone threw another piece of wood on the fire, the sudden surge of fresh flames caught her in a scarlet halo, illuminating her flashing eyes, deepening the fierce colour in her cheeks. 'I have never betrayed you—not even in my thoughts.'

'I saw you in Siward's arms!' The cry came from Gy, no longer able to contain himself. 'The day Roger Chabret came to Wynterfold, you were with him in the Great Hall. You begged him not to leave you.'

Siward half turned as if to start towards the squire, and found his way barred by two burly men, both armed with swords and thick staves. Rollo's gaze rested on him for a moment before returning to Alisandre. She looked puzzled, as if she did not recall the incident.

'Have you nothing to say, Kutti?'

'Whatever the boy saw—or thought he saw—is beyond me. I will not lower myself to his base level by answering,' she replied haughtily. She stiffened as Rollo indicated that the boy should continue, and her piercing gaze centred on his face as he opened his mouth.

'That was not the only time I saw... He has held her, my lord, I swear it! One day I saw her weeping on his shoulder...'

'I do not deny that,' Siward said bleakly, 'but what exactly did you see, boy?'

'You were holding her close, like... It was not proper!'

'Were her arms about my neck? Was she kissing me? Showing me some of this affection you say we have for each other?' Siward demanded.

'I—I... It is as I said...' Gy faltered under Siward's unwavering gaze. He began to grow hot and uncomfortable as faces turned in his direction and he became the focus of attention. It had all seemed right in his mind when he had related it to Lord Rollo. They had been friendly—more than friendly. 'Lady Alisandre seemed—overwrought... She was clinging to you.'

'Clinging to me? I thought you said *I* was holding *her* in my arms? What would have happened, do you think, if I had not been holding her?'

'I don't understand. Why are you trying to twist my words?'

'Am I? I was holding a tearful woman in my arms. That is true—trying to ease the grief she was experiencing at the news the man she loved, her husband, was dead...foully murdered. Had I not been holding her, she would have collapsed. As she did indeed collapse in the chapel. Do you remember that, Gy? I carried her to her room, accompanied by her maid. Not alone!'

'Enough! The boy's loyalty has always been with Lord Rollo. If he misunderstood . . .' Alisandre lifted her slender shoulders in a shrug of acceptance. 'I shall never forgive him this day, but perhaps he thought he was right.'

'Is he right in his assumption that Siward spent a night in your bedchamber?' Rollo flung the accusation at her without warning.

'No!' she gasped, appalled by the question.

'I saw him,' Gy cried. 'And that was not the only time. And I heard him say things to you! He came to you when Chabret was confined in the dungeons, and I heard you talking. I listened at the door, and I'm not ashamed to say so. He was saying he realised how he felt about you when he rode with you in the foothills near Shah'mat.'

Alisandre caught her breath, her whole body stiffening with shock. Rollo's heart sank as no words of denial sprang to her lips. He held out the horn of wine, and she took it with shaking hands and drank. His fingers brushed hers as she returned it, and she flinched from the contact as if her skin had been seared by a red-hot flame.

Rollo hurled the horn from him with such force that it smashed against a tree and fell to the ground, shattered. He sprang to his feet, his hand on his sword, glaring down at her, pushed beyond endurance by her continued refusal to repudiate the accusations showered on her.

'Well? Your life hangs by a thin thread, woman. Defend yourself!'

Alisandre looked up into his murderous features, and met the glittering eyes with a calmness that sent a whisper of surprise through the onlookers. An innocent woman would surely have defended herself, somehow? And a guilty one would have blustered, perhaps wept, or thrown herself on the clemency of her husband. This one did neither. It was as if she held the whole proceeding in utter contempt.

'I have nothing to say. Do with me what you will.'

'*I* have something to say.' Siward's hand reached for the hilt of his sword, before realising it had been taken from him. 'Your spy speaks the truth, my lord. I lied to you. I told you she was naught but a friend. For her, that is still so, but not for me. I do love her. It was never my intention for her to know it, but— but I am not as adept at concealing my feelings as you are, my lord.' There was a sneer in his words, a challenge on the scarred features. 'I was in her room that night, but you have only my word, as my lady refuses to speak, that we are innocent of your squire's suspicions. It is true also that I spent a night in her bedchamber.'

'Siward! When?' Alisandre gasped, stunned by the revelation.

'The night of your nightmare, my lady, when you dreamed that Lord Rollo stood at the foot of your bed. We should have believed you, shouldn't we? I persuaded you otherwise, even though I found evidence of someone being not only in your room, but in the nursery. Is that where you hid, my lord, while we scoured the house for an intruder?' Rollo did not answer, and Siward continued relentlessly, driven by forces he could no longer control in his desire to free Alisandre from her terrible plight. 'Such behaviour is beyond my comprehension. A man of honour, a knight, to deceive his own wife into accepting that he is dead, while he dallies with another woman! To leave her alone and unprotected against those he knew would use her for their own ends. That kind of love I do not understand. The kind I bear her demands that I protect her from all who would harm her, and this I will do. I remained in her bedchamber all night after her maid had managed to soothe her back to sleep with a strong sleeping-potion. She will confirm my words, should you wish,' he added with heavy sarcasm.

'Did you see my wife's maid?' Rollo demanded of the squire.

'No, my lord. Only Siward, as he left the room. I could not see inside,' was Gy's reluctant answer.

Rollo tore his eyes away from his wife's face and stared moodily down in to the flickering flames at his feet. She had looked shocked—as if she had known nothing of the incident, he thought, and then her face had become closed to him and to those watching again, wiped clean of all emotion. 'Is it a fight you want, Siward?'

'She has the right to have someone to defend her,' Siward said coldly. 'Give me my sword!'

'In the Holy Land, she had me. Now, she has you. I wonder who will come after us, eh? Chabret, perhaps? One of John's puppets, married to her so that Wynterfold will be for ever within his grasp? If you want her, you must fight for her, as I did...'

Helpless to intervene, her path blocked by the same two men who had menaced Siward, and with others about her she knew would restrain her if she tried to stop this terrible thing, Alisandre was forced to watch the two men circle each other, warily at first, then engage and draw apart, testing their strength, their skill, in slow, unhurried movements that made her want to scream for it to end. But when it did, one of them would be dead.

Rollo lunged forward, the firelight gleaming on the blade that sliced through the air towards Siward's shoulder. He deflected the blow, then staggered back, clutching his weapon with both hands. His movements were clumsy, and faltering, not those of an accomplished fighter. His heart was not in it, she knew, but not to defend himself fully! She had never seen him fight two-handed before. Even at the quintain, he would swing his sword with expertise and use only his right hand. Why two... Her gaze fastened on the fingers that clutched the hilt—awkwardly, she realised, as though they were stiff, or had no strength. That was why he covered them with his other hand. *She* had done this to him! Her dagger had sliced his hand, and because of it, he could no

longer use it properly. And yet he had chosen to fight
Rollo, to sentence himself to death in the hope of
saving her! Such was the love he bore her.

A scream was ripped from her lips as Rollo sent
Siward's sword flying, and she saw blood oozing between his fingers. Not from any fresh wound that had
been inflicted, for the blade had not touched him, but
from the reopening of the recently-healed scars across
his palm. 'No more! Can you not see he is hurt?' she
cried pleadingly. 'For the love of God, let him live!'

'You are asking for his life, Kutti?' Rollo turned
and saw that the blood had ebbed from her cheeks.
What more proof did he need that she cared for this
man more than for him? 'I have not touched him—
yet!'

'If you do, it will be the most dishonourable thing
you have ever done in your life,' she breathed. 'He
cannot defend himself. His hand is—is crippled. Look
for yourself!'

Siward's wrist was caught in a grip of steel, the
fingers prised open to reveal the two long gashes that
had been opened again by the weight of his sword.
His eyes met those of Rollo's, and in them there was
no plea for clemency—only a silent challenge.

'Enough!' Rollo thrust him away with a contemptuous gesture that hid the shock of Alisandre's
words, the realisation he had almost killed a man
unable to defend himself. 'You are a fool! She is not
worth dying for. No woman is.'

'Once you thought so,' Siward reminded him. 'I
am no less a man than you when it comes to pro-

tecting those I love. You should not have told him,'
he said, his gaze reproaching Alisandre as she came
to him and used the silk scarf at her waist to bind his
bleeding hand. 'I did not wish it.'

'Nor do I wish you dead. Have you finished with
us, my lord, or do you have more—entertainment—
planned for your men this evening?' Alisandre asked
with a scathing look.

'You have chosen how it will be,' Rollo snapped.
'Take him! He is all you will ever have, Kutti. I shall
make sure of that. In the morning you can return to
Wynterfold.'

'Why did you tell him?' Siward repeated.

They had been escorted to the hut and left alone.
No one seemed interested in them any more,
Alisandre thought, noting the absence of a guard at
the entrance. But where would they go if they escaped
but back to Wynterfold, because Jarl was there, and
Rollo knew it? He was letting them go, but she did
not understand why. She turned and stared at Siward,
who lay on the rough pallet of straw, the only sparse
comfort the hut provided, nursing his injured hand.
He was in pain, yet she knew he would have willingly
continued with the fight, had Rollo insisted. 'No one's
blood shall be shed on my account,' she replied
quietly.

Siward relaxed back on the pallet, his eyes closing.
She had made him drink several large horns of wine
as she tended his wound, and it had made him drowsy.
He yawned, tension slipping away from him, forced

his lids to lift again and allowed his gaze to dwell on
the smiling woman who stood watching him.

'Where is my wife? Where is Alisandre?' Rollo's
voice somewhere above him jerked him brusquely
back to reality. Siward struggled upright, blinking into
the flare the other held. The hut was full of shadows,
but she was not there! 'What game do you play now?'

'I must have slept . . .' Siward cursed himself for accepting the wine. His hand fell to his belt and discovered that the knife was missing from its sheath.
He came up on to his knees, awkwardly because of
his hand, then to his feet, saying hoarsely. 'My
knife . . . Find her! Quickly!'

'What are you saying? That she means to harm
herself?' Rollo gave a bitter laugh. 'She has no reason.'

'You have given her one tonight! You have taken
life from her! No, she will not harm herself, though
once she did try, and I stopped her. Had I known I
would bring her to this in doing so, perhaps I would
not have wrested the knife from her. . . my hand would
be whole, and I could have sunk my blade into your
black heart, my Lord of Darkness! No, she will not
use the knife to plunge it into her heart . . . For a
woman of her courage, a more terrible course of
action has been chosen. Find her!'

Siward's words followed Rollo out of the hut, and
he sank on the straw again, knowing that whatever
took place when Rollo found her was not for his eyes
or his hearing.

*   *   *

Alisandre slipped unnoticed from the hut. It was growing late, and those who had not taken themselves off to sleep were stretched out about the fire, where one man stood guard, but his back was towards her and she passed close by him without a sound.

Clear moonlight guided her as she picked her way through the bracken and the thick trees. She had no thought of trying to escape. Rollo was going to set her free in the morning, and the last hope in her had died with his words. He did not believe her to be innocent. The bright moon was obscured for a moment as a cloud passed across it, and almost simultaneously an owl somewhere screeched in alarm and flew off to a safer sanctuary. Something rustled in the undergrowth as a night animal foraged for food. Even now, she was not alone.

Taking Siward's knife from her sleeve, she reached out for a handful of loose hair. The blade was sharp, her strokes swift and deft. She wanted to be rid of this crowning glory that he had mocked. It would be as she had promised. No man would ever touch her, or see it, as he had. He was dead . . . She was alone again. . . Tears blurred her vision as the locks of tawny gold hair fell on to her skirts, and rolled unchecked over her cheeks as she gritted her teeth and continued to cut relentlessly. She was sobbing now with frustration, rocking to and fro as she fought in vain to contain the bitter memories sweeping over her, which in turn were followed by those of tenderness and love, recollections of great passion and utter contentment. How could he allow it to end as if it had meant nothing to him? To her, he had meant everything. To him, loyalty to his kind had come first and foremost... Women came a bad second, and were of little importance. The Lord of Darkness was not a man to be dismissed lightly from the mind, or easily forgotten. No, she would never forget!

Her head felt strangely light... Her trembling fingers touched the hair shorn close to her head. It was done. Now let him mock her!

'Kutti!' The harsh whisper came out of the darkness in front of her, and the knife fell from her limp grasp towards the figure who came to fall on his knees before her. 'He said you had tried to kill yourself once before. I thought... Never this!' His shocked gaze searched her tear-streaked face, a hand tentatively touched her wet cheek, then reached higher to lace his fingers through the closely-cropped hair. 'Why this? Why now?'

'My husband is dead. It was a vow I had to keep. Why should you care? I am nothing to you. Go away and leave me in peace.'

'Peace!' His laugh was bitter. 'Do you think I have had one moment's peace since I left you? If you do, you are a fool.' His hand dropped to her shoulder, and immediately he felt her tense as his fingers bit into the softness of her bare skin. 'No more will you have peace when you leave here. No man will ever rouse you as I did...'

'But my life will be my own,' she flung back, with reproach in her voice. 'I shall be my own mistress.

No one shall take from me what is mine. I shall not be betrayed by those I trust—and love!'

'I have never made love to Margaret. Just once I tell you this: we were never lovers! Did her lies turn your mind—is that it? You sought to revenge yourself on me for something I had not done? I thought you to be a woman who would stand by her man, no matter what!'

'Woman!' Alisandre echoed, and across her young face flashed an expression of such pain that he felt as though a knife had been twisted deep inside him. 'I am not a woman; you said so yourself to Margaret and indicated it to others. I am a child—an incapable child who cannot manage her own affairs. That is why you gave her that paper...to oust me from Wynterfold! I shall never forgive you. Never—never!'

He seized her by the shoulders and roughly shook her. His blazing eyes burned into her very soul, confusing her with their intense wildness. He looked for all the world as if he cared, but he did not! If she allowed him to use her again... If she gave way to the longing rising inside her, the desire to sink against that broad chest and beg him to hold her and kiss her... No! No!

'I gave her nothing.'

'You lie! As you lied to me at Wynterfold. She shared your bed! I found her handkerchief beneath your clothes on that morning she left with Prince John.' The words were flung at him, despite the increasing pressure of his fingers biting into her shoulders. Then one arm went round her waist, the other gripped the nape of her neck, forcing back her head. His face came close to hers, and his glittering eyes made her quiver.

'I was drunk that night, Kutti! I remember nothing after you left me, and I wrote some letters. I drank myself insensible, because I was too proud to come after you and drag you back to my bed—by your hair, if necessary...' His voice trailed off, and he groaned as he realised what he had said. 'If I had, perhaps we would not have come to this. Tamir ibn Dak was right. I was born under a dark star. I destroy all I touch.'

She lay silent in his arms, drained of all resistance by his nearness. She closed her eyes, and felt a tear force its way beneath her closed lids and slowly cross one cheek... felt his lips gently trace its path to the corners of her mouth. Margaret had lied about so many things. What if he had spoken the truth? Not lovers? His lips seared hers, parting them hungrily with a desperation that brought a low moan from her lips. If she submitted now... Yet how could she not? He was everything to her! Without him, her life was empty... a shell without a centre or a heart.

'Rollo!' His name broke from her lips, barely audibly, and she felt his arms tighten about her. She was pressed close against his chest, and the scent of horses came once again to her nostrils to remind her of the times he had ridden away from Wynterfold early in the morning and come back while she was half-asleep to claim her. Her fingers clutched at his tabard, seeking proof even now that this was no dream—no terrible nightmare from which she would awake and find herself alone. 'Are you real? Are you flesh and blood? You came to me that night—I know you did!'

'How could I not? I needed to see you—to be with you.' His lips buried themselves in the nape of her neck, and she clutched him closer to her. If she was damned to the eternal fires of hell for these few moments, she would willingly accept the sentence. 'You called my name in your sleep...' He had not meant to touch her then—or now, but, as before when he had stood in the shadows watching her toss and turn in restless sleep, he was unable to contain the longing to hold her in his arms, possess the soft mouth that uttered his name and soothe away her fears.

'In my nightmare, you stood before an open grave, beckoning me. I thought I had failed you in not joining you,' she murmured, and he lifted himself back from her to look down into her face.

So calm. So serene. She had accepted death to be with him. If only Siward's love were not between them, how easy it would be to look on her now and believe her innocent of all his suspicions. Why had she not sent Siward away when she discovered he loved her? To keep the man at her side, so close, tempting fate and provoking gossip! Rollo knew he should not have allowed memories from the past to intrude on to this present life, this idyllic existence he had shared with Alisandre. Yet once the thoughts and suspicions had returned to his mind, there was no turning back. He was a man lost—a man without a heart! He had nothing to live for without her, and despite all he had been told, he still wanted her desperately. That would never change.

'Siward said you tried to kill yourself—that was how he injured his hand. Is it true?'

'He has broken his promise...' she gasped. 'Yes, it is true. He wrested the dagger from me, and was hurt. I shall never forgive myself for what I have done to him. You could have killed him!'

'If he means nothing to you, why should that matter?' he demanded, his eyes narrowing sharply as they searched her face for some sign that might betray her feelings.

Her steady gaze met and held his as she answered him. 'He is my friend, and yours. I shall never turn my back on him, as you have, or allow others to force me into sending him away. He has stood beside me through many difficult times. Had he not been so vigilant in his protection, I should have been raped by Roger Chabret. Your friend, Will Appleton, will confirm that I speak the truth. He was there.'

'I sent him to the village to learn what was happening.'

'Then it was *you* who attacked Chabret and stole the money he was taking to Prince John! And, because of it, he took out his spite on the village. He allowed his men to have free use of the women. He is an animal!'

'And they paid for it, did they not?' Rollo reminded her. 'As for Chabret, he and I will meet again—across swords! He will never live to wed you, that I promise.'

'Are you telling me I must say nothing of this— that you are alive?' Alisandre whispered. 'If you have proof of Margaret's attempt on your life, then face her with it! And Chabret! Prince John would be made to listen to you. Don't make me go back to Wynterfold alone? If you must stay in hiding, let me share this existence with you. I am not afraid. I do not want to be alone again.'

'You shall never be alone, Kutti.' Rollo's tone was harsh, and he heard her catch her breath at the admission.

'No, never! Even when I thought you dead, you were still with me.' Alisandre pressed herself against his chest once more, seeking comfort from the arms which slowly enfolded her and began to caress her body. 'You were in every room, beside me at night . . . sometimes,' she gave a shaky little laugh as she added, 'sometimes I could hear you breathing, even though I knew you were not there. I should have known nothing could ever truly part us.'

'Can it not, Kutti?' She gave a low moan of pleasure as his fingers loosened the fastenings of her gown and drew it away from her shoulders. In the bright moonlight, her skin gleamed like alabaster. Her eyes were wide, gleaming with a brilliance that took his breath away. A half-smile played round her mouth as she undid the ribbons of her shift and drew it open. This night was hers! She would show him that nothing had changed between them. Let him send her away then!

'Kiss me, my husband and then tell me you will abandon me to the lecherous arms of Roger Chabret! If you can!' she challenged.

'No other shall ever have you!' Rollo swore as he pressed her down beneath him, his lips searing hers with angry, passionate kisses that made her senses reel and clamour for more. He ran his fingers through the short hair framing her face, cursing her for a futile gesture that would not blind him to what had been seen and heard about her, and, in the same breath, whispered tender endearments as his mouth travelled down over her throat and shoulders to her breast.

She had won, Alisandre thought in exhilaration as she abandoned herself without shame to the ecstasy of his touch, all else forgotten. They were together again. Together!

CHAPTER THIRTEEN

ALISANDRE awoke to find herself still lying beneath the shade of the huge oaks where Rollo had carried her after they had made love, his cloak wrapped about her body. She lay looking up, watching the sunlight seeking to find a way through the dense foliage until, at last succeeding, it slanted across the bed of bracken that he had made up for them both. It had been reminiscent of days long past on the journey to Jerusalem, where she had been forced to sleep in the open beneath supply wagons, sometimes on the hard earth. He had never been far away. Last night his body had cradled hers the whole time, as though he were frightened that if his arms no longer held her, she might slip away into the darkness. He must allow her to stay now! Nothing had changed between them.

She sat up to smooth back her hair, and her fingers came in contact with the ragged ends clustered about her face, halting them with the shock of recollection. She had cut it! Rollo had surely understood the desperation which had driven her to such an act, for he had not condemned her. It would grow again, and once more he would run his fingers through it, watch her as she braided it, as he had done so many times before.

'My lady...' Cerdic was standing at her side, his mouth gaping as she turned and he, too, realised what she had done. She smiled and rose to her feet, holding Rollo's cloak close against her breast.

'Where is my lord?' She hated no one this morning.

'He sent me to fetch you.'

'Is there somewhere I can wash?' she asked, her heart beginning to race. Her gown was creased, and her hair... Perhaps she could do something with it before he saw her again. She felt the colour rise in her cheeks as she looked down at her gown and shook the dirt and leaves from about the hem. If she appeared like this, everyone in the camp would know what had happened between them!

'There is no time, my lady. The horses are saddled and waiting, and you are to leave at once. Thomas and I are to escort you and Siward back to Wynterfold and to remain, should you require us.'

'Leave? I don't understand...' The colour that had tinted her cheeks and given them a healthy glow to match that in the depths of her blue eyes vanished and her hands clutched the cloak more tightly.

She began to run towards the camp, heedless of her cropped head or the dishevelled condition of her clothes. Hampered by her long skirts, she tripped and fell, but before Cerdic could reach her side to help her up, she had scrambled to her feet and continued her headlong flight down the slope to the main camp, barely pausing for breath.

Four horses stood waiting. Siward and Thomas Luckett were already mounted and waiting. A few feet away from them, his hands on his hips as he surveyed the path before him, stood Rollo. At the sight of the woman who came running towards him, he tensed himself for their encounter. He had no choice but to send her back to Wynterfold. She would be in no danger there with the Guard to protect her. They would watch Margaret de Greville-Wynter constantly, allowing her no chance to wield any power in the house. If there was so much as a hint of trouble, he would know of it within the hour. And he would personally take care of Roger Chabret! He would pay with his life for daring to lay hands on the wife of the Duke of Aquitaine. One day Margaret, too, would face his wrath, and he would settle with her for the attempt on his life. A few more months would free him from this outlaw existence. God willing, Richard would by then have returned to the shores of England, and he himself could leave them to return where he rightfully belonged.

'Why are you sending me away?' Alisandre's determination to contest his decision wavered as he fixed her with a cold stare. Nothing in his face betrayed what they had shared not a few short hours before. 'I will not go!'

'You will. I do not want you here.' Do you not know what would happen to you if this camp is raided by Prince John's men? he wanted to shout at her. If you were not taken as a hostage, they would use you as Chabret once tried to do—your title would not save you. But the words, which might have made her understand his motives and the courage it took him

to stand before her and see the misery in her eyes
without wavering, did not pass his lips. 'Go, before
I change my mind, Kutti. You are free of me if you
wish.'

She recoiled from the harshness in his voice, the
bleak, pitiless features. Her fingers fluttered trembling to touch a wisp of a curl that had crept against
one cheek, and the reproach in her sapphire eyes was
more eloquent than the crudest oath she could have
hurled at him. Never would he be forgiven for this
final insult! He had used her for the last time.

'I shall go.' She forced the words through stiff lips.
Dropping his cloak to the ground at his feet, she
turned away, offering her hand to Cerdic, who helped
her to mount her horse. For a moment Rollo's gaze
was centred on the rope of twisted gold and the
sapphires glinting in the sunlight on one slender hand.
'Have no fear that I shall betray your secret. This place
does not exist for me, nor what happened here between us. My husband died many weeks ago, and is
buried at Wynterfold. One day soon, I pray I shall
accept that in my heart. Free? Would that I could be,
but you ensured last night that that can never happen!
Your dark star has touched me for the last time . . .'
Her voice faltered and broke, and even as he started
forward as if to grasp her bridle, she wheeled the horse
about and urged it at a rapid pace through the camp,
scattering people to right and left of her.

Cerdic was not far behind, but Thomas Luckett remained to escort Siward. The Norseman came close
to where Rollo stood, his gaze still following

Alisandre's departure even though she had been swallowed up from his sight amid the heavy undergrowth.

'I shall take her from you if I can,' he vowed.

'Then learn to use your left hand, my friend, for the next time, I will surely kill you. And no matter what has passed between us here, that would grieve me,' came the deadly answer. No matter where she went or who was at her side, she would always belong to the Lord of Darkness!

'Are you sure you want to do this?' Alisandre asked anxiously, and Siward nodded gravely. Immediately upon her return to Wynterfold, she had ordered the two chests belonging to Rollo to be prised from their hiding-place under a loose flagstone beneath the altar in the chapel, where they had lain hidden since Roger Chabret's visit, and loaded on pack-horses. Once they were in Rollo's possession, she could safely leave this place—and England. She would leave, taking only her own belongings with her. In one of the chests she had placed all the jewellery he had given her, including her wedding ring, and now wore only the heavy silver bracelet encrusted with precious stones that had been upon her arm when Rollo had found her in the prison cell at Acre. It was another reminder of those far-off days when her life had been uncomplicated by emotion, when she had been her own mistress, not subject to the demands of a husband and family. Those days will come again, she told herself. She would put her life with Rollo behind her. He no longer wanted her—or his son. Jarl was her life now!

An hour before sunset, she stood in the courtyard and watched Siward lead the pack-horses out through the main gate, biting her lips so that she would not call him back and give him a message for the man she would never set eyes on again, yet whom she knew would haunt her dreams and plague her life with bitter-sweet memories for as long as she lived.

Jarl was having his first riding-lesson, held in front of Thomas Luckett on the back of the most docile horse in the stables. The reins were put into his hands, and he beamed proudly, waving to Alisandre, who waved back and smiled, some of her unhappiness receding at the sight of him so content. Of course he would miss a father, but she would more than make up for that. She had enough love for two, and he would always be surrounded by friends. He would lack for nothing, she told herself. The sooner they left Wynterfold, the better for them all.

She was turning to go back into the house when the sound of horses approaching caused her to look back towards the gate. Siward was barely out of sight on a distant slope. Margaret! She recognised the pennant of her men at arms immediately. And, beside her, Roger Chabret! They had lost no time in returning to assert their authority!

She did not wait to greet her cousin and the man who accompanied her, but went directly to the kitchens to tell the cook of the new arrivals and have an additional room prepared. When she returned to the Great Hall, she found that Roger Chabret had already summoned wine to be served and was waiting for it impatiently. Margaret hurried past her out of the room, her face red with anger and muttering something under her breath that she did not catch.

'Lady Alisandre, I was wondering if you were trying to avoid me. You do know that is impossible, don't you?' There was an edge to Chabret's voice, as he took her hand and touched her fingers to his lips, lingering over the caress until she snatched them away in disgust.

'You are not welcome here, you know that,' Alisandre said icily, withdrawing to a seat across the table from him while a servant poured them wine. 'But there is nothing I can do about it.' She fought down her dislike of this man, and he gulped back the first goblet without appreciation and motioned it to be refilled. 'And my cellars will be empty if you continue to drink like that.'

'Then I shall refill them—as a betrothal gift.' His narrowed gaze mocked her defiant words. 'No, there is nothing you can do about it, Alisandre. No more can Margaret. I shall have you, Alisandre, and no one in this land shall stop me. There is not a man alive who could!'

There *is* one, Alisandre thought, as she drank her wine, but he no longer cares for me. Rollo had sent her back to Wynterfold, knowing that she must marry Roger Chabret on John's order, or proclaim that he was alive! In doing that, she would be condemning him to certain death at the hands of Margaret's men or those of the Prince. To remain silent would mean domination by this grinning ape who sat opposite her, slowly undressing her with his bold eyes. But only if she remained at Wynterfold. She must allay not only Chabret's suspicions, but those of Margaret. If she were to have any chance of escaping, both must believe that she had lost all courage and will-power to oppose the royal order.

'As you say, sir—I shall learn. I am sure you are an apt teacher, and many years ago I was taught that obedience brings its own rewards.' She watched his eyes narrow even more at her quiet words. Carefully, she thought. Not too quickly, lest he become suspicious. 'I have no liking for this match, as you well know. I need time to accept it, and you. I have just lost my husband!'

'I shall soon make you forget him,' Chabret returned sardonically.

'In time, perhaps. I pray you, sir, have patience.'

'Patience!' He came to his feet and was behind her chair before she could move. His hands closed over her shoulders, then moved down over her bodice to cup her breasts. His lips descended on the nape of her neck, warm, wet, nauseating as they travelled round to her mouth. For a long moment she was forced to endure the pressure of them grinding into hers, while his hands explored her body as if she was some breeding-mare at an auction. She shivered with disgust as he drew back, and rose to her feet, trembling from head to toe, her cheeks ashen. Thank God Siward had not been here to see her so mishandled!

'Well may you tremble, woman! The months will pass slowly—too slowly.'

'I must go and greet my cousin...' Alisandre cried, and fled from him, with his mocking laughter following her up the staircase. She had no intention of going near Margaret, but the door was open, and her cousin called to her as she passed.

Reluctantly, she came just within the threshold, demanding coldly, 'What is it? I have things to do.'

'You look as if you are out of breath, Alisandre. Running from Roger, by any chance? Perhaps you and I should talk awhile.' Margaret motioned Alisandre to a chair, but she shook her head. 'Very well. I offer you a solution to your problem. You no more want to marry the man than I want you to. So perhaps arrangements could be made whereby he would disappear from the scene, leaving you free?'

'And, in return, I give you Wynterfold?' Alisandre said. 'What do you mean—he would disappear? How? If anything happened to him, I would be the first suspect and you the second. I trust you not, cousin.'

'With good reason.' Margaret showed no annoyance at the insult. Time was on her side, but not on Alisandre's, for Chabret was not a patient man. 'Give me Wynterfold and go back where you belong—to Shah'mat—and take that Norseman with you. You are still young; you have all your life ahead of you. There is nothing to keep you here in England, is there?'

'No,' Alisandre conceded, 'there is not. But—murder?'

'What are you talking about?' Margaret gave a soft laugh, concealing her triumph that Alisandre had not refused the offer outright. She was more afraid of Chabret than she admitted . . . and with good reason. 'My hands have never been tainted with the blood of others. I was thinking of an accident . . . The story is more likely to be believed after the unfortunate attack on the Lord Rollo. Do you not agree?'

'I—I want to trust you . . .' There was a convincing tremor in Alisandre's voice that brought Margaret to her feet. She was half-way to achieving her goal, she suspected . . . and decided that she would lose nothing in being generous.

'You are thinking of Rollo. Listen to me, Alisandre. I have a confession to make, and you must believe I speak the truth. I was jealous of you, my dear. You know how it was when I was young. I have not changed . . . I still use people.' She watched Alisandre's eyes widen in disbelief at the words. Never before had Margaret been so open with anyone! 'Your husband never betrayed you. When you saw us together that night, I was kissing him . . . and he laughed in my face. I hated him then, and I wanted to hurt him—and you. I wanted to see you at each other's throats. If I cannot have something I want, no one else shall have it.'

'But . . . the letter he wrote?' Alisandre whispered brokenly.

'A marvellous copy, I am sure you will agree. From time to time I make use of a craftsman in Winchester who can produce anything I ask—for the right price. As for the seal, I took it from your bedchamber and had it copied. Within a day, it had been returned without being missed. It was all quite simple, my dear—and so effective. Of course, if you should not accept my help, I shall deny this conversation. You would not be believed; you know that.'

'Why—Why are you telling me this—now?' Rollo had not lied to her! He had said they were not lovers, and she had not believed him. 'You spent a night with him here, and at the coast you were together... You told me so.'

'I lied.'

'Why have you told me this?' she repeated.

'To show you what I am capable of doing when I set my heart and mind to it. I shall free you from Roger Chabret, if you wish, and you will give me Wynterfold and leave England.'

'Yes.' Alisandre said dully. 'Yes, I wish it.'

'You show remarkable good sense for once, Alisandre. There will be no wedding, you can take my word for that.'

'No, there will not.' And, somehow, before she left these shores, Alisandre would expose her cousin to the world for what she was: a liar and a cheat, a murderess! And then at least she would have gone a little way to compensate for the harm she herself had done to the relationship she had shared with her husband.

If only she had believed! If only he had believed in her! Now it was too late for them both.

Rollo stared down at the small casket he held, and the expression on his face was terrible to see. He lifted blazing eyes to the face of the silent man who stood watching him, and demanded bleakly, 'What message came with these?' Everything was returned to him— everything. Even her wedding band; the sapphire necklace and earrings; her rubies; the belt of beaten gold woven with gems. Only one thing... Yes, one thing was missing, he realised. Had she forgotten to include it? Or was it significant that the object not returned was the brooch he had had fashioned for her in Winchester. His emblem and hers, joined as one. Why should she keep that, of all things?

'With those, my lord, there is no message,' Siward replied. 'The chests I bring come with the compliments of the Lady of Shah'mat!' His words—not hers.

'How dare she...' Rollo almost choked on his words. A reminder of what they had shared?

'How so? It is her right to use the title, the more so now, as she will soon be back there with your son,' Siward added firmly. 'Once there, you will have lost her.'

'Because you will be there with her?' Rollo's mouth deepened into an ugly smile. 'The road to the coast is long and dangerous. Perhaps you will never reach your ship safely.'

'I have no intention of returning with her, although she does not know it yet. Perhaps another—more suited—will be at her side.' Siward reached beneath his tabard, and immediately three men flanked him, their hands on their swords. The brief flicker of a smile which crossed his scarred cheeks was full of bitterness. 'You have good men, here, my lord, who are worthy to be your Guard. As I was. As I still am, crippled or not. Take these, read them, and perhaps you will understand the woman who weeps for you still at night. On the night she attempted to take her life, she wrote these. One is for me. I have nothing to hide. Read it,' he urged, as Rollo stared frowning at the papers he held. 'Her only concern was for her son, that he should be raised in peace, by the most learned men in the land. No thought for herself. Nothing was important to her that night, except that she joined you in death. Is that the act of an adulteress? Her love almost destroyed her. You achieved what that failed to do. Even now she is forced to entertain Chabret and the Lady Margaret at Wynterfold because it was Prince John's command. She remains silent because to reveal that you are alive would bring down his hounds on your head and turn this woodland into a wasteland. No one would be spared in the hunt for you, my lord. I shall stay, because you may need someone close at hand that you can trust.'

The words were meant to bite deeply, and they did. Rollo's narrowed gaze searched his face. 'Better that

I am not with her, or I might forget who and what I am. Better that I do not see her every day to remind me. She will have others.' Will she have you? Siward wondered, as Rollo's attention was once more directed to the letter. The words leapt up at him:

> Forgive me if I cause you pain by what I do, but without my husband, I have no reason to continue in this world. You have honoured me with your friendship and your companionship, and you have greatly honoured me with your love. I think you always knew I could not accept it. Give it to some fortunate young woman whom you will take as your wife. Give her all that you would have given me, and she will be the happiest woman in the land. Care for my son...

'Wait!' Siward paused beside his horse, his hand falling to his sword as Rollo's voice rang out behind him. He turned, and realising the uselessness of the gesture—even if he could have used his weapon skilfully, he was still outnumbered—allowed it to fall back to his side.

'You say Chabret and Margaret have returned?'

'As I was leaving to come here. They did not see me. I hid until they were almost at the gates of Wynterfold. I did not want Chabret's greedy eyes on those.' He nodded towards the full chests he had brought. 'He will not be pleased to know he has been outwitted by the Lady Alisandre for a second time. I must return at once. I may be able to help her.'

'And what use will you be with only one hand?' Rollo snapped, and angry colour flamed into Siward's face.

'At least I shall not turn my back on her when she needs me,' he retorted, and both men eyed each other in silent antagonism. They both wanted the same woman, yet one was willing to give her up for love— the other out of distrust and bitterness. Each loved her... Rollo wheeled about, shouting orders, and men went racing for their bows and full quivers of arrows. Horses were quickly saddled.

'No more shall I. Not again!' Rollo stretched out a hand, but then withdrew it, shaking his head. 'I have no words now; my mind is in confusion... I have brought pain to those closest to me—to you, to her.'

'None are necessary, my lord. I am at your command, as always,' Siward answered without resentment.

'Can you not be at my side, as you used to be? Before my pride and my loyalty to others destroyed what we once shared?' This time Rollo's hand remained outstretched, and into it Siward placed his own, wincing slightly at the iron fingers which closed over his. One again—as in battle! His victory was a hollow one, for he had lost everything except the friendship of the two people who were most important in his life. Friendship was not love, but without it what was there for a man such as he?

'I shall accompany you, my Lord Rollo.'

The quiet voice that came out of the shadows behind them brought both men wheeling round. Rollo had thought her still resting before continuing the journey to Winchester. He marvelled at the great stamina of this old woman of seventy-one, whose unfailing courage in the face of hardship and cruelty had commanded his respect and devotion since he was a lad of thirteen.

'You have risked much for me—and for your king. Now it is time I repaid you. Your work here is done. It is time you took that lovely wife of yours back where you belong. I shall not accept your refusal—and I *shall* provide the funds for Verduse. The king will approve of that. He would not wish either of you to suffer because of what you have done for him. You will be in France to greet him when he returns.'

In silent homage Rollo and Siward knelt before Eleanor of Aquitaine. One man preparing himself to do battle—to the death if need be—to regain his lost love. The other accepting the cold touch of death's hand upon his shoulder, for that very morning had he not heard the croaking of a raven? His time had come.

Alisandre felt weak with relief when Siward returned. He had been gone so long that she was certain Rollo had after all decided to exact some terrible revenge on him. The man bowed before the table, barely acknowledging either Roger Chabret or Margaret, and apologised for the lateness of his return with the excuse that his horse had gone lame on its way back.

This would be the most plausible explanation for his absence, he had thought. Before he could retire, Margaret waved to the servant beside her, indicating that a chair should be placed beside her. To Alisandre's surprise, he did not refuse. Was he deliberately trying to antagonise Chabret, she wondered, not liking the way the man glared across the table?

'Alisandre, my dear, you are preoccupied.' Chabret leaned towards her. 'Perhaps you are trying to remember where you have hidden the other chests of money—and also silver plate, if I remember rightly.' The look Alisandre gave him made him draw back, his eyes narrowing at the derision on her face. The bitch! What had she done?

'They have gone, sir. Delivered into safe hands where they belong,' Siward replied.

'She's sent them for Richard's ransom,' Margaret laughed heartily. 'Well done, cousin! So that was the reason for Siward's little journey.'

'As you surmise, they have gone,' Alisandre replied quietly. What had Rollo thought when he had opened them and found her jewels? she wondered.

'I would that you act so painstakingly when you are in my service,' Margaret murmured, and felt a flicker of alarm when Siward fixed her with a cold stare, his mouth deepening into a smile that mocked her words.

'Your service! I told you once that I would as soon go to bed with the devil's daughter as make love to you. Besides, I do not want to end up in a grave, like Lord Rollo.'

Alisandre's hand flew to her mouth. What was he saying! If either Margaret or Roger suspected they knew of their involvement in the attempted assassination of Rollo, their lives would be worthless! Perhaps they already were.

'I know not how or where it was planned,' Siward continued, 'but I do know they were Sir Roger's men. With you behind the scheme, I suspect. He does not have the brains, or the courage cold-bloodedly to plan a murder. Like your brother Hugo, he prefers to knife men in the back. He does not like to see how they look when they die.'

'You go too far!' Margaret hissed, half rising to her feet. She slowly sat down again as Chabret began to chuckle, the sound jarring her taut nerves. This was not how it should have been. She should not have been the one made uncomfortable, with cause to fear for her life. 'You know nothing! You have no proof!'

Alisandre caught her breath so sharply that all three at the table turned to look at her. She could feel Rollo's presence! Now she knew, with a sudden racing of her heart, that he had returned to Wynterfold.

Siward smiled—a sad, haunted smile that was to linger with her long after the horrors of the night had passed and love and happiness were once more hers. 'You are about to have returned what you thought you had lost for ever, my lady. With my blessing, for what it is worth to you.'

She could not speak . . . there was a tightness in her throat, as her eyes searched the shadowy alcoves.

'Am *I* proof enough, Margaret?' The voice came out of the darkness of the stairwell, and brought Margaret to her feet with a choked cry. 'It was one of your men who spied on me at the coast, followed me to my ship and reported back to you, was it not? You knew then that I never had any intention of going to Verduse. He overheard sufficient to gather that I was a courier.'

'Who speaks?' Margaret's voice trembled as she searched the shadows, and then, as the tall figure stepped into the light of the wall torches and his face was illuminated, she reeled backwards, a scream rising in her throat. 'You are dead! You are not the Duke of Aquitaine. You cannot be!'

'Why? Because you have gazed on the body I sent back, and satisfied yourself that he was the right height and build, that the jewellery he wore was mine, that the remains of the leather guards about his wrists hid scars like these.'

Rollo thrust his hands out towards her, revealing the twisted scar tissue about his wrists from the heavy shackles that had kept him a prisoner of the Saracens and which had always been covered by two wide strips of dark leather. His pale eyes glittered as she sank slowly into her chair, and flickered past her to Roger Chabret, his hand frozen upon the table as he reached for his goblet of wine.

'I have come to kill you, Chabret. Not so much for the cowardly attack you and your men perpetrated on me, but for your attack on my wife. Did you really think she would ever belong to anyone but me?' There was a deadliness in the soft voice that told the man he would be shown no mercy.

Alisandre could not move, could not speak, as Rollo came down the last four steps towards the table, a hand upon his sword. He did not look at her; all his attention was focused on the frightened face of the man who rose trembling from the table, blustering . . .

'It was not my idea, it was hers!' Chabret flung out an accusing hand in Margaret's direction. 'My men, yes, but *she* planned it. She wanted you dead because you sent her away. She would have killed your wife, too, if I had not stepped in to ask Prince John for her hand. I saved her life!'

'Be quiet, you loose-mouthed fool!' Margaret jumped up and slapped him soundly across one cheek. 'Kill him, and then there will be no witnesses. Your men can take care of these other two. Kill him, I say, or we shall both taste the hangman's noose!'

She wheeled away from him towards the door, her voice shrill with fear as she summoned her men at arms. Cerdic pushed her firmly back to the table with a contemptuous oath.

'Your men have all been taken care of, my lady,' Siward told her coldly. 'And his. Disarmed, and locked away where they can do no harm. Nothing shall prevent justice being done here tonight.'

'Where did you get men?' Margaret began wildly. She was trapped by the web of her own lies and left with only a coward and a braggart to defend her. He would not be able to defend himself against the Lord of Darkness; there was death in his eyes. No mercy would be shown to either of them. She could not die! And then she saw Alisandre's smile, and the colour ebbed from her cheeks. She had known he was alive! 'Will Appleton! And you!'

Rollo nodded grimly. His sword cleared its scabbard as Chabret made a sudden move, heaving the table away, scattering wine and crockery about the floor and momentarily blocking his path.

Chabret turned to run, and found his way blocked by three determined Guards, was forced to turn back, but at the sight of the blazing features of the man who came relentlessly towards him, his nerve failed. 'Mercy! I will tell you everything.'

'Draw your weapon, or I will kill you where you stand!' Rollo threatened.

'Kill him, you coward!' Margaret screamed. 'With him dead, there are no witnesses against us. I shall be believed, not these Guards, his men who would lie for him.' She was shaking with fury, and fear also. When Roger had been dealt with, it would be her turn!

'There is one witness you cannot silence,' Rollo growled, stepping slightly to one side, and her eyes flew to the staircase and the slightly stooping figure who leaned against one wall. 'Do you think Prince John will believe your word over that of his own mother, who has heard with her own ears of your treachery—and his?'

Margaret rushed past him like a wild-eyed animal towards the spot where Queen Eleanor stood. What was in her mind, no one knew. Siward leapt forward to intercept her, but almost instantly she wheeled about, and Alisandre cried out a warning as she caught the sudden brilliance of a razor-sharp blade. It flashed down towards Rollo's unsuspecting back—but it never reached its mark. Instead, it sank deep into the chest of the man who thrust himself between her and the man he had sworn to serve.

Before Alisandre's horrified eyes, Siward slumped to the floor, and with a snarl of rage, Rollo caught Margaret's wrist, twisting the weapon back upon herself. In that brief instant as she struggled against him, a thousand shattering memories exploded in his brain. The fire that had almost ended his life on the way back to Wynterfold, her doing! The lies and pain Alisandre had been forced to endure, because of her! His own torture, his marriage in ruins, his son almost a stranger to him. For what? Loyalty? Honour? Pride? Love had not entered into it, and it should have been the factor that ruled his life.

Contemptuously he thrust her away from him, and growled harshly, 'I want to see you swinging from a rope, my lady, beside your lover! Death will come slowly. I want you to suffer as you have made others suffer.'

'Never!' Margaret's hand moved so swiftly that he had no time to stop the dagger sinking into her breast. She fell to her knees, swaying as she regarded the faces fading before her vision. Alisandre, kneeling beside Siward, trying desperately to stem the flow of life-blood ebbing from him, and knowing it was hopeless. The Norseman's face was so peaceful...even in death he mocked her, because she was dying and she did not want to... He did not care! He had saved Rollo! Roger Chabret, ashen with terror. She had wasted so much time on that one. A smile touched her mouth as her eyes came to rest on Rollo's merciless features. He alone showed no compassion for her. He wanted her dead—it was etched deeply there for all to see. And then she laughed, and Alisandre trembled at the sound, recognising in it a desperation such as the woman had never shown before, and fear that in her own life she had often instilled in others without experiencing it herself. 'I have destroyed you! I may die, but I have destroyed you, and you have destroyed them with your jealousy and hatred. I have deprived you of your wife and your best friend. Nothing will ever be the same for you again. They were innocent! Innocent! Never again will two people love you as they have—or be so loyal to a man not worthy of the sacrifices they so willingly made. My brother is avenged at last!'

She fell forward on to her face among the rushes already stained red with spilt wine. No one moved to touch her. Without a word, Rollo flung himself down beside Alisandre, his fingers covering those which tightly grasped the Norseman's crippled hand. She lifted her eyes to his, bright tears welling. She could not speak, yet she wanted to say so much...

'Do not put me in the ground for the worms to feed upon, my lord. Send me to Valhalla with a sword in my hand, like a warrior,' Siward begged, stumbling over the words as blood rose in his throat to choke him.

'Yes, old friend, it shall be so. I swear it,' Rollo answered, feeling a wetness about his own eyes, and caring not who saw it.

'Siward,' Alisandre whispered, but the hand in hers grew lax, slipping from between her nerveless fingers. Weeping, she turned her face into Rollo's shoulder, but he did not touch her. It was Eleanor who came forward to lift her gently to her feet and draw her away.

'Let me help,' Alisandre begged as Rollo lifted Siward in his arms. Never before had she seen such open emotion on his face. His pride was shattered. He staggered slightly with the burden, but shook his head as the Guards advanced as one man to help him. The pain in the eyes which looked at her tore at her heart. Not only pain, but guilt, she realised. His life had been saved by the very man he had unjustly maligned and accused of betrayal.

'No, alone, I must do this for him. I have to make my peace with him, don't you understand?' Blindly Rollo turned away past the Guards without seeing them, out through the open door and down the steps to the courtyard. Alisandre flew after him, but dared follow no further than the steps, and watched in silent misery as he strode through the throng of villagers and men at arms clustered there and passed without a backward glance out through the main gates.

'Where does he go?' she whispered, not knowing who could give her an answer.

'He goes to pay homage to a friend, my lady, and to do his bidding. In the old days, the body of a dead

Viking warrior was laid with great ceremony in a boat and sent out to sea. Flaming arrows would set it ablaze, freeing the spirit from entrapment in the earthly body so that it could safely reach Valhalla, the Hall of the Slain, the domicile of all brave men who fall in battle. And there was no braver man than Siward. Somehow, my Lord Rollo will perform this last service for one who has served him faithfully— he has sworn it.'

From the window of her bedchamber, Alisandre watched the grey curling smoke spiralling skywards. The flames of the pyre that had consumed Siward's body had long since died down, but Rollo had not returned to the house, and her concern for him was mounting. She had not slept at all, but watched him first from the solar and then from this higher window after escorting the Dowager Queen to a room where she could rest. Little conversation had passed between them, except when the older woman had taken her in a motherly embrace and promised to make all well again between Alisandre and her husband. Verduse would be rebuilt at her expense, she said, and they would all, Jarl included, come to court, where Rollo's activities would be made known. Richard's ransom was all but raised and would soon be on its way to Worms. When he was free, there would be more honour for Rollo. Perhaps another title, and lands for their son.

Alisandre's words of thanks were half-hearted. How could he refuse such generosity? And Jarl's inheritance would be secure. How could *she* refuse? Even though it was not what she wanted.

There was no sign of Rollo below. Her eyes searched the sea of faces in the courtyard without finding him. She could wait no longer; she had to go to him. Without thought for her undressed hair or the creased gown still stained with Siward's blood, she hurried downstairs and out into the early morning air. It was barely light, and the lack of activity at an early hour, when servants were usually stirring to go about the day's work, was instantly noticeable. This would not be a pleasant day for anyone, she thought, her mind momentarily dwelling on her dead cousin who had been carried to her room and prepared for burial in the family graveyard that afternoon. She did not mourn the passing of someone so evil, nor did she feel any elation that Roger Chabret had been taken bound and in disgrace to face Prince John at Winchester. At his side, to exonerate herself and Rollo from all charges that might be brought against them concerning his activities while with Will Appleton, was the Dowager Queen Eleanor, the one force John could not and dared not oppose.

At the gate, Rollo sat with his back against the high encircling wall, his shoulders hunched like a defeated man, his head between his hands. He seemed unaware of Alisandre until she went down on her knees before him and gently touched his arm. He had stripped to the waist as he laboured to build the pyre, sweat pouring from his body as he cut and piled brush and heavy wood, and carried Siward's body attired in a clean tunic and hose to lay upon it. At his side, he had placed his sword and the very few belongings that the man possessed, and alongside these a fine silver chalice so that he could quench his thirst during the journey to Valhalla, and food to satisfy his appetite. Across his chest, he had laid the shield he had always carried in battle. Then he had put a torch to it, and stood with the heat of the flames upon his half-naked body, yet not feeling them, only the deep burning pain in his heart, that he knew might never leave him.

The eyes lifted to Alisandre's were dull and red-rimmed from the smoke, which also blackened his face and skin. His hands were cut in places, grazed raw, and the blood had dried on them.

'Oh, Rollo, my love,' she whispered, laying her head upon his lap.

'Get up! Don't ever kneel to me again, woman! I am not worthy,' he rasped harshly, and she raised her head with a wan smile.

'You are my lord—my master—my husband. You will always be so. I shall never leave you, my own true love.'

'I am what I am, Kutti.' Tentatively, as if afraid of her reaction, his hand closed over her arm and drew her closer. 'My so-called love almost destroyed you. Can you live with that—with me and my jealousy? I shall always bristle when another man looks at you— I shall not be able to help it, but I shall try not to show it. I swear I shall never—never—hurt you again. Was she right? Have I lost you as I have lost Siward?

Is it possible that her hatred has destroyed what we once shared?'

'The pain of what has happened between us will pass,' she promised. 'We have so much to be grateful for, and to look forward to in the years ahead. We have Jarl and each other, and you are destined for great honour. The Dowager Queen has told me of her intention to rebuild Verduse for you, and that is what you have always wanted.' She would accept anything, so long as they were together.

'No!' The fingers curled about her arm tightened painfully. 'No! Verduse is part of the past. It is not for us. For Jarl, maybe, one day, but not for us.' He looked up at the brightening sky as if only then aware that it was day. 'Queen Eleanor will return from Winchester soon, and we must make our own preparations to leave.'

'To leave?' Alisandre echoed. To go where?

'We are to journey with her back to France, and then . . .' Rollo looked into the pale face watching him with a growing expectancy in the depths of those blue eyes. Hope was rising there as they searched his face, and he felt a sudden peace settle upon him. It was over! He was done with his black pride, never again would it rule his life, disrupt this wonderful existence that he shared with her. They would return where they belonged, and it would be as it was before. Long days of harmony and contentment, endless nights of unbridled passion, of undying love. His gaze returned again to the smouldering embers of the fire. 'When it is cool, I have one last thing to do: to gather up his ashes. They will be scattered upon the open sea. His soul and spirit have gone before, and they will follow, and he will be reborn again and reunited with his ancestors. No words, however well meaning, can erase what I have done to you, Kutti. I can only beg your forgiveness. I loved you too much...I always shall...' His voice broke, and he lowered his head so that she would not see the agony in his eyes, his fear of rejection.

Alisandre's hands cupped his face, and gently raised it. Her lips on his were warm and soft, restoring life in him. With a groan he gathered her tightly against his chest, devouring the sweetness of her mouth with fierce, bruising kisses that left her breathless and in no doubt any longer of his love.

'Will you come with me?' he whispered against her hair, not daring to look into her face lest he saw even the slightest hesitation before she answered, which might tell him that happiness would not yet be his. 'Will you come back to Shah'mat? We need no others about us. I want only you by my side, and Jarl. I want to make love to you day after day after day, night after night ... until you say you forgive my stupidity. My terrible stupidity!'

For a moment Alisandre was still against him, and his heart almost stopped beating in panic, then she drew back, and he saw the brilliance in her eyes, tear-drops sparkling like diamonds amid the sapphire pools, as joy overwhelmed her at his words.

And then, as she looked up at him, other words came drifting to her on the morning breeze. Did he

hear them, too? 'You are about to have returned to
you that which you thought you had lost for ever.
With my blessing, for what it is worth.' Siward's words
were like a holy benediction, bringing peace once more
into their turbulent lives. Their worth was beyond de-
scription. No mere words could evaluate his gift, given
not out of loyalty, but from love for them both. In
sacrificing not only that love, but his life, he had ensured that their own would once again blossom.

'Yes, my love,' she whispered. 'Oh, yes! I shall
come with you.'

BETRAYALS, DECISIONS AND CHOICES...

BUY OUT by David Wind   £2.95

The money-making trend of redeveloping Manhattan tenement blocks sets the scene for this explosive novel. In the face of shady deals and corrupt landlords, tenants of the Crestfield begin a fight for their rights – and end up in a fight for their lives.

BEGINNINGS by Judith Duncan   £2.50

Judith Duncan, bestselling author of "Into the Light", blends sensitivity and insight in this novel of a woman determined to make a new beginning for herself and her children. But an unforeseen problem arises with the arrival of Grady O'Neil.

ROOM FOR ONE MORE by Virginia Nielsen   £2.75

At 38, Charlotte Emlyn was about to marry Brock Morley – 5 years her junior. Then her teenage son announced that his girlfriend was pregnant. Could Brock face being husband, stepfather *and* grandfather at 33? Suddenly 5 years seemed like a lifetime – but could the dilemma be overcome?.

These three new titles will be out in bookshops from MAY 1989

W❍RLDWIDE

AROUND THE WORLD WORDSEARCH
COMPETITION!

How would you like a years supply of Mills & Boon Romances ABSOLUTELY FREE? Well, you can win them! All you have to do is complete the word puzzle below and send it in to us by October 31st. 1989. The first 5 correct entries picked out of the bag after that date will win **a years supply of Mills & Boon Romances** (*ten books every month - worth around £150*) What could be easier?

R	D	N	A	L	R	E	Z	T	I	W	S
E	O	N	M	C	H	I	N	A	A	C	C
G	M	U	I	G	L	E	B	N	N	U	O
Y	E	C	E	G	W	H	I	Z	C	B	T
P	D	R	H	S	E	R	I	A	Z	A	L
T	N	S	M	P	E	R	U	N	D	D	A
N	A	W	I	A	T	P	I	I	E	N	N
Y	L	A	T	I	N	A	N	A	N	A	D
N	G	S	T	N	H	Y	D	E	M	L	Q
W	N	O	J	A	M	A	I	C	A	L	A
R	E	L	A	D	A	N	A	C	R	O	R
T	H	A	I	L	A	N	D	D	D	K	H	I

ITALY	THAILAND	SCOTLAND	SWITZERLAND
GERMANY	IRAQ	JAMAICA	
HOLLAND	ZAIRE	TANZANIA	PLEASE TURN
BELGIUM	TAIWAN	PERU	OVER FOR
EGYPT	CANADA	SPAIN	DETAILS
CHINA	INDIA	DENMARK	ON HOW
NIGERIA	ENGLAND	CUBA	TO ENTER

HOW TO ENTER

All the words listed overleaf, below the word puzzle, are hidden in the grid. You can find them by reading the letters forward, backwards, up or down, or diagonally. When you find a word, circle it or put a line through it, the remaining letters (which you can read from left to right, from the top of the puzzle through to the bottom) will spell a secret message.

After you have filled in all the words, don't forget to fill in your name and address in the space provided and pop this page in an envelope (you don't need a stamp) and post it today. Hurry - competition ends October 31st. 1989.

Mills & Boon Competition,
FREEPOST,
P.O. Box 236,
Croydon,
Surrey. CR9 9EL

Only one entry per household

Secret Message _____

_____

Name _____

Address _____

_____

_____ Postcode _____

You may be mailed as a result of entering this competition